UNDER THE GREEN STAR

by
Lin Carter

ILLUSTRATED BY
TIM KIRK

*With an Epilogue by the author
on the "Burroughs Tradition."*

DAW BOOKS, INC.

DONALD A. WOLLHEIM, PUBLISHER

1301 Avenue of the Americas
New York, N. Y.   10019

For Tom Anderson,
who loves an
old-fashioned yarn.

FIRST PRINTING 1972

Table of Contents

PART IV.   THE BOOK OF SLIGON THE BETRAYER

Part I

THE BOOK OF
CHONG THE MIGHTY

Chapter 1

THE BOOK FROM TIBET

As I sit writing these words, a weird sensation of unreality sweeps through my being.

Beyond the bay window before which my desk is drawn I can see green fields and tall trees—hickory and mountain laurel, pine and yellow poplar. And beyond those fields and hills lies the waking world, filled with busy and teeming cities, with ordinary people who lead everyday lives—lives that seldom touch on mystery and marvel.

Which is real—the fantastic adventure I feel compelled to relate—or the world beyond my windows? Have I only dreamed that I have stood where no man of my race has ever set foot before, or is this dull world of tax returns and ball-point pens, of air pollution and TV talk shows, itself but a dream? Are both worlds real?

Are—*neither?*

Perhaps I could begin my story in earliest youth, when wide reading brought the first intimations of the occult within the reach of my speculative imagination. But—no— I shall begin this narrative with the first moment I took into my hands that immeasurably ancient and incredibly precious book from the secret heart of Asia.

The long-dead hand that inscribed these yellowed and wrinkled vellum pages in queer crooked characters called this book the *Kan Chan Ga.* For a thousand years it lay in a jeweled box of gold in the most secret archives of the holy Potala—the Temple-Palace of the Dalai Lama in hidden Lhasa itself. Before that . . . no one can say for certain. The Commentaries say it was found in a prehistoric stone tomb in the foothills of the Trans-Himalayas long centuries before even the first God-King ruled from the Lotus Throne—but no one really knows. There were empires before Egypt, and cities older than Ur, and the sages whispered of lost lands and forgotten realms long before Plato dreamed of Atlantis and set those dreams down to excite the imagination of men forever.

The title, *Kan Chan Ga,* is not Tibetan. Neither are the odd, crooked little rune-like letters wherewith the vellum pages are thickly lined. The Commentaries say the book is written in Old Uighur, a language that was forgotten before Narmer the Lion brought the Two Lands together under one crown and ruled as the first Pharaoh. And certain obscure and ancient texts hint there was once an Uighur Empire amidst the trackless sands of the Gobi in Central Asia . . . long, long ago when all that desert was a blooming garden, before the Poles changed. I neither know nor care.

The book cost me two hundred thousand dollars and seven years. When holy Lhasa fell to the invading hordes from Red China, and the Dalai Lama fled into exile in India, the *Kan Chan Ga,* and certain other priceless treasures, were taken into hiding. In those confused, horrible days, when the snowy peaks of ancient Tibet were crimson with the flames of burning lamaseries and scarlet with the blood of murdered sages, the book was lost. It was to have traveled west with the Panchan Lama and his retinue, but in the snowstorms, with the roar of machine guns echoing from the rocky cliffs, one party of lamas went astray. The book was hidden in the crypts beneath a minor lamasery of little consequence, from which, after years of searching, my agents found and rescued it.

And now I held it in my hands ... the book that the most ancient sages speak of with awe and reverence as The Key of The Liberation of The Soul. ...

My father invested wisely and well in the Market and left me with a private fortune large enough to permit me to indulge my curiosity in the occult sciences.

I am thirty years old, tall, broad-shouldered, deep-chested, and strongly-built. I have blond hair and gray eyes and am accounted a handsome man. But strength and health and handsomeness are a mockery to me, for since I was six years old I have not taken a single step without the help of mechanical aids.

All my father's fortune could not purchase a cure for polio in the twenty years before the perfection of the Salk vaccine.

Being a cripple, it was perhaps natural that I should turn my attention inward. The lore of the occult attracted me from my earliest youth. I had the finest tutors, and mastered Latin, Greek, Sanskrit, and Hebrew. The ancient Eastern science called *eckankar*—soul-travel, the projection of the so-called "astral body"—fascinated me. In my search for the secrets of this lost art, this forgotten science, I went far. A thousand books hinted of the secret, but none could reveal it.

In that strangest of all books, the *Bardo Thodol,* I first heard of the old book in Uighur. The *Bardo Thodol,* which may be described as a geography of the travels of the soul after death and before birth, whispered of the *Kan Chan Ga.* Crumbling scrolls from an old abandoned monastery in the Sinkiang province of China, smuggled out through Hong Kong, told me more. A hundred agents searched the Orient at my behest, and at length the book was unearthed. The seventh of the "living gods" of Tibet— the Gupcha Lama himself—translated the Uighur for me, on my promise that the sacred book would be returned to the Dalai Lama once I possessed the wisdom that I sought. This has now been done.

I read the translation of the odd, crooked characters with an inner excitement that my reader can only dimly imagine. If the secret lay in these ancient pages, then I, who had not taken an unaided step in twenty-four years, could travel the earth as swift-winged as thought itself. Unseen, I could walk the thronged bazaars of Rangoon—peer up at the smiling enigma of the Sphinx by moonlight—gaze upon the carven stone ruins of jungle-grown Angkor Vat—explore the mysterious ruins of elder and cryptic Tiahuanaco amidst the plateaus of the Andes.

Bit by bit, the secret emerged from the strange manuscript. Man is more than body and mind and soul, the nameless sage of the Gobi had written. His nature is sevenfold: the animal flesh, the material body itself; the vitalizing life-force that animates that flesh; the ego that is the conscious "I" of every man; the memory, that contains a record of all that each man has seen and felt and known: the astral body, the vehicle of the higher soul-levels on the second plane; the etheric body, that is the chalice contained within the astral vehicle; and, seventh and last, the immortal soul itself, that is the precious flame within the chalice.

Subtly linked together are these seven selves, which make up the individual man. In deep sleep or in hypnotic trance, the astral body sometimes ... *wanders* ... causing strange dreams of far-off places and visions of distant friends. But only a stern discipline can release the etheric body and the soul it contains, together with the conscious ego. *That* was the secret I had sought so long; and I stood upon its threshold at last.

Night after night, mind-weary from the occult disciplines I had practiced, I lay in my bed and stared wistfully up at the stars. If I could master the ancient art of soul-travel, no more would I be chained and earthbound, locked in a helpless, crippled prison of flesh. I would be *free* ... free as few men have ever been ... and how I hungered for that freedom!

Day after day I practiced the inner concentration, the "Loosening of the Bonds." Few even of the holy sages of old Tibet had ever in truth mastered *eckankar*—but few of them had been driven by the motive that goaded me on.

I shall not bore my reader with a description of my labors. Nor shall I tell of the heartbreaking moments of failure and despair that overcame me at times. The task was long and arduous ... it is no easier to train the

muscles of the body to Olympic skills, than to train the
mind and soul and spirit in this occult science. But at last
the day came when I deemed myself ready for the experiment.

Having fasted and performed certain austerities and
calmed my mind with the recitation of certain *mantras,* I
informed my housekeeper that on no account was I to be
disturbed, and locked myself within the upper portion of
my ancestral house which served as my private quarters
and library.

The good woman was accustomed to this sort of behavior. My quarters were equipped with a kitchenette and
pantry, and many times in the past I had secluded myself
for days on end behind locked doors while busied in my
researches. I impressed upon her that she was not to
interrupt me for any reason.

Emptying my mind of all trivial thoughts, I stretched out
on a soft, comfortable sofa and composed myself as if for
slumber. Closing my eyes, I visualized a black sphere. It
hovered before my mind's eye exact in every detail, almost as if it were a material object. My concentration was
focused upon that orb of darkness with such intensity
that, ere long, I was unaware of outside sounds. Then I
began to will myself into the deepest trance. I began to
lose all awareness of my own body; all outer sensation
faded; no longer could I feel the faint brush of moving air
against my face, or hear the beating of my own pulse, or
feel the pressure of my crippled body against the soft
fabric of my couch. All of my attention was turned
inward now.

Next I visualized the black sphere as not a globular
object, but an illusion—I saw it as the black, circular
mouth of a tunnel, and down that endless tunnel I imagined myself traveling, until I was swallowed up in unrelieved darkness.

Deeper and deeper I descended, until at length I perceived the faintest spark of light ahead, like a star against
the breast of the night, like the far, dim opening at the
end of the tunnel. I drifted toward it at ever-increasing
speeds, until I seemed to hurtle through the black hollow
darkness at an inconceivable velocity.

I emerged from darkness into dim ruby light.

For a moment I could make nothing of my surroundings. I seemed to be enclosed in a rectangular box of considerable depth, whose floor was drowned in deep gloom and whose upper levels were awash in faint red luminosity.

Then, with a strange, tingling shock of surprise, I recognized my surroundings. I was in the very room wherein I had immersed myself in the sleep-like trance ... but *floating near the ceiling!*

Many hours had passed, for early afternoon had given way to the hour of sunset, and the last level beams shone redly through the windows of the western wall.

Gazing down from my height I saw ... *myself.*

I lay stretched out on a couch, my arms folded upon my chest, my face waxen-pale and curiously unfamiliar to me. It came to me then that I had never before actually seen my own face as others saw it, but always in a mirror or through the medium of some other reflective surface. Always before I had seen my face *reversed,* in reflection: but now I saw myself as the rest of the world saw me. It seemed a trivial difference; but it was oddly stranger than it should have been. My face was ... *empty*; blank and expressionless.

Was this because I lay in trance-like sleep, and all of my facial muscles—which in my waking moments were in tension, giving my features what we call "expression"— were now completely relaxed? Or was the strange blankness of my features due to the fact that my body was now—*untenanted?*

I cannot answer now, nor could I then.

Curiously, I turned my gaze upon my own being, and found that to the eyes of my immaterial self I was an invisible spirit. Indeed, now that I began to accustom myself to this peculiar state, I felt oddly unaware of myself in every way. A man in the flesh may strip himself naked and yet be aware of his bodily envelope in a thousand small ways—the roughness of a carpet against his bare soles—the chill wind blowing against naked flanks—the thousand little internal sensations of the body, tongue resting against teeth, dryness of throat, an itching finger. None of these I felt in my new spirit-state: it was as if I did not possess a body at all.

And, of course, that was the truth of the matter.

I had liberated myself from my body.

I was—*free!*

Chapter 2

BEYOND THE MOON

To the windows I—*drifted*. I know of no other term whereby to describe the mode of locomotion I employed. I did not stride or even swim through the air: I ... *moved*. In my bodiless state, the whim was father to the deed. I but thought of going over to look out of the window, and found myself there without any sensation of having propelled myself thither.

I gazed out. The sun was all but gone now, mere guttering embers burning amid the distant pines. Suddenly, I wanted to be out in the open air ... and again found that I had traversed an interval of space with no sensation of having physically moved. I hovered far above the lawn, which lay drowned in darkness below. Had I been here in the body, I should have experienced the giddiness of vertigo; now I felt nothing. I hung in the air thirty feet above the wet grass, but it was like a *dream* of flight, rather than the physical experience.

A sudden intoxication seized me: I could go anywhere—do anything! I rose to a great height with the swiftness of thought. The hilly Connecticut countryside lay spread out beneath me, fields and forests and the checkered farms with their sown fields. The rooftops of the nearest community, Harritton, were visible from my height; I could see the white steeple of the Congregational church, the yellow marquee lights of the cinema, the red neon sign of the Cozy Oak Bar and Grill, the luminous funnels of moving headlights along the highway leading to New Haven.

At this height—in the flesh!—I would have felt intense cold, the pressure of great winds—but I felt nothing. Nor

13

could I hear a sound, not even the beating of my own heart or the faint hollow roaring of blood moving through the arteries of the inner ear, that seashell sound that is the closest to absolute silence man ever knows.

Why should I be able to see and not to hear? True, I was as immaterial as thought itself, and sound waves passed through me without the slightest obstacle—but was not this true of light waves as well? And it was truly light by which I saw, not the ghostly luminance of some astral sun, but the light of the ordinary world. Why was I opaque to light, but transparent to sound or matter? The ancient pages of the *Kan Chan Ga* said nothing of this. And to this day I have no explanation to offer; I can but set down exactly what I experienced, and leave it to others wiser than myself to explain.

I looked down. The woods bordering my property lay below, all but invisible in the darkness. Within those woods was a narrow stream by whose banks I had played as a child before polio struck me down. A whim bore me there without the slighest sensation of motion. The darkness under the overhanging pine boughs was inky, but the moon was beginning to rise and a dim silver radiance pervaded the place. The stream was wider than I remembered, and the banks more deeply cut—but that should be the case, considering the years that had passed.

A fat raccoon was washing its food in the gliding waters. I watched it with delight. Had I been present in the body, the wary little fellow would have vanished in the bushes on the instant: now, although it paused, to rear up and peer around with bright eyes gleaming in its comic, black-masked face, it showed no sign of being aware of my presence.

Like this fat, furry little inhabitant of the woods, I, too, was—free! I could go where I would, and no walls or barrier of steel could hinder my passage.

Behind me, in the great house, my body lay in deep sleep. My heartbeat had slowed by this time, my body temperature had dropped, and my breathing was shallow. To leave my body far behind would not cause it harm in any way, so the *Kan Chan Ga* assured me. Were I to spend hours, or even days in this insubstantial state, I could return to my body in confidence that it had suffered in no way from the departure of its tenant. In the deep trance state in which it now lay, the fires of life burned very low. There were minimal demands on that store of vitality in this state; to remain away for days or even weeks would not mean that I would return to find a gaunt, starved corpse.

Nor did my exertions while in this astral state cause any drain of energy. I was essentially disembodied thought—free spirit—and I drew upon cosmic sources of energy as yet unstudied by Western science.

The moon was rising now; it glowed like a shield of pure silver through the black branches. A sudden heady intoxication seized me—I could travel wherever I might—to the very moon itself, if the whim pleased me!

But, no—men of my race had walked the desiccated powdery plains of that shining sphere—why should I, in the perfect freedom of my spirit-state, go where other men could travel?

I gazed beyond the moon to where the ruddy spark of Mars burned like a dim coal—*Mars!* The goal of the human imagination for untold centuries—I could travel there, if I willed, with the unthinkable swiftness of thought itself! What matter the vast distances of interplanetary space: a million miles or eight millions are naught to the unleashed spirit!

Upon the very thought, my soul lifted with joy. To walk the surface of another planet—to go where no man of my world had yet been in all the ages of infinite time! Vague thoughts of the books I had read with such fascination in my boyhood came back to me—memories of old Edgar Rice Burroughs and his unforgettable Martian adventure classics—now I, too, like John Carter, could stride the dead sea bottoms of mysterious and romantic Barsoom!

Again, the whim was father to the deed. In a twinkling the Earth vanished beneath me and the blackness of space closed about my being. The moon flashed by in a dim dazzle of gray-silver, and the blurred red sphere swam up before me until it filled my vision. I drifted down toward it like one in a dream, and slowly came to rest on an illimitable dim plain of dry red sand and crumbling porous rock.

About me, stretching to a horizon that seemed strangely closer than Terrestrial horizons, I stared through the dim twilight of the Martian day. The sun was only a fierce, scorching, and intolerably brilliant star at this vast distance, and it shed little light on the red desert and the low ancient hills.

I gazed up, searching for the famous twin moons, and at length I found them. They were very much smaller than I had thought they would be, and very dim, almost invisible. I looked beyond them to the Earth I had left behind, and found it, a dim, remote blue star with a minute silvery companion.

Then I stared down at the dim-litten red sands beneath me. I sought to bend and touch the sands, but I had no bodily awareness at all and do not know if my spirit-self performed the action or not. This is very difficult to describe: I was not *aware* of having arms wherewith to reach, or a waist wherefrom to bend; and all that chanced was that my "level" sank until "I" was closer to the ground than before.

I next ascended and floated above the endless plain, searching for some feature—either the legendary canals the early astronomers had seen, or had thought they had seen—or the immense craters NASA had photographed from Mariner.

I saw neither . . . instead, I saw—*a city!*

Excitement flamed up within me, and I sank toward it.

It lay in the shelter of encircling hills, and the red sands lapped up to drift about its squares and to sift slowly into the streets. I stared about me with heartaching wonder. A city of tall, impossibly slender, incredibly graceful fluted towers with flaring tiers and swelling domes, all fashioned from some unknown and glistening stone, like pale golden marble, faintly veined with green. There were broad avenues and mighty forums and long shadowy arcades of slim columns, and on the slopes of the encircling hills, facing upon what had once been a broad seashore a billion years ago, were the husks of lovely villas.

I drifted like a ghost through the deserted city, wondering what sort of beings had dwelt in these empty palaces and what dreams they had dreamed, gazing up at the cold mockery of the stars. And in a small square I found at last a likeness of the long-gone dwellers of the seaside metropolis, and gazed with wonder upon the slim, graceful statue of palest alabaster, that limned the likeness of a race that had died before the first Terrestrial mammal had risen from the primordial slime.

It was manlike, slender and impossibly tall, with a

featureless oval for a head. Two of its several boneless limbs were lifted to the skies, and the smooth casque of its face was tilted on its long graceful neck, as if it stared up longingly at the stars it could never reach.

At the base of the statue was an inscription, but in no tongue known to me, a lovely, elaborated script full of curlicues and flourishes.

I turned from the slim, mournful, lovely thing restlessly: this city was a necropolis. Here reigned Death and only shadows drifted through these silent streets. I wandered on, floating above the domed villas, and through the column-fronted palaces, and found murals filled with the slender, faceless beings posed against fantastic gardens that had withered to dust aeons ago. Not even a bone had been left untouched by time.

Beyond, on the stone quays where once the blue waves of a forgotten sea broke in sheeted foam beneath the hurtling glory of the moons, I raised my sight to the stars that blazed like strewn diamonds on black velvet, far clearer and more brilliant than those that glitter through the watery atmosphere of my own world.

If I could traverse the abyss between the worlds, the stars themselves were not beyond my reach, and I had no fear of becoming lost in the star-sewn immensities of the universe, no fear of traveling so far I could not find my way back to that shell of flesh that lay slumbering on Earth. For the mere act of wishing my return would cause it, even if I had no conception of distance or direction.

So again I lifted up my sight ... and a strange green star caught and held my attention.

Green it was, that distant spark, as a flame of emerald, and it blazed down steadily from its height as if beckoning to me ... as if calling me from the illimitable vastnesses wherein it hung.

Why this particular star, out of the millions that jeweled the Martian night, seized my attention I cannot say. Perhaps it was only that green is a rare hue for stars and that I could not recall having ever seen a star of this strange color before. Or there may have been some other and far stranger reason for the fascination which now seized upon me—and of this I shall speak at another time and in another place.

Suffice it to say that floating there amid the impossibly slim towers of the Martian city, I was rapt and held by the flame of emerald green that blazed above me through the night. And I thought to myself—why not?—mere distance is no hurdle to a bodiless spirit—I could circumnavigate the Universe itself, if so I desired.

And I soared up from the barren surface of Mars and left the ghostly city behind me to its shadows and its immemorial memories, and flew out into the greater universe that lay beyond.

By now all conception of time had left me. In this bodiless spirit-realm, both time and space—distance and duration—were without real meaning, and I discovered that the awareness of passing time is only a habit of the flesh-bound consciousness, no more.

Thus I cannot say whether my flight to the Green Star was as swift as a flashing instant, or occupied some duration. I was not aware of any slightest sensation of motion. The dim red disk of Mars shrank and vanished beneath me; the fierce star-like beacon of the sun dwindled and was lost in the jeweled mists of clustered stars that gemmed the night. I flashed on through darkness in a strange dream-like flight and it may have been an aeon—or an instant— before the Green Star swung before me like a tremendous globe of vernal flame.

For a long moment I floated there in space before the terrific orb of furious light.

Then a world swam into view out of the darkness—a planet, like the one whereon I had been born, or the one from whose surface I had flown hither, an instant or an aeon ago.

On sudden impulse, I directed my flight toward the dim silvery orb whose surface was wreathed in lacy mists. Down through its atmosphere I flashed . . . down to the surface of a new and unknown world . . . and into an adventure more strange and perilous and thrilling than any other man has ever lived!

Chapter 3

WORLD OF THE GREEN STAR

And I found myself in the midst of an astounding scene, unlike any surroundings I had ever seen before.

Imagine a world whose skies are a dome of dim, pearly mists, through which but faintly a sun like a sphere of incandescent emerald blazes.

A world of colossal trees—trees which loomed about me on all sides—trees of such unthinkable girth and height that beside their like the titanic Redwoods of California would dwindle to saplings—trees that must have towered *two full miles* into the misty, luminous air!

I had come to rest an enormous distance above the surface of this strange new world. Near me soared the vast bole of a tree taller than many Earthly mountains. Its trunk soared aloft, hidden from me by innumerable branches of comparable size—branches as broad as six-lane highways—from which burst an infinite number of strangely yellow leaves larger than men.

Below me, the trunk of this forest titan dwindled thousands of feet down until it also became obscured and finally concealed by the tangle of immense boughs and the thickness of innumerous leaves. I could see perhaps half a mile in every direction, but everywhere I looked my vision eventually ended in masses of pale yellow leaves or entangled oak-like boughs of enormous size. I felt like an ant amid Sequoiae, or a mote floating among the towers of Manhattan.

The rays of the Green Star above the mists shone down through the immense foliage whose yellow leaves filtered the light into a strange dim green-gold gloom.

In this mystic half-light I began to perceive forms of higher life. Perhaps six hundred feet from where I hovered, a scarlet reptile with a saw-toothed spine clung with sucker-feet to the underside of one colossal bough thrice the breadth of Broadway. The scarlet lizard itself was the size of twin Bengal tigers.

I caught a flicker of movement below me—a twinkle of jeweled brilliance, the glitter of gold, the sheen of sheeted opal—and in the next instant my attention was riveted upon the most fantastic steed and rider imaginable.

The steed was like a dragonfly—but larger than a Percheron. Four long narrow oval translucent wings flickered in the currents of air ... wings like thin slices of glassy opal, veined with crawling threads of glistening jade!

A head like a glittering helmet of burnished gold, crowned with branching antennae of crimson velvet, soft as down; and, for eyes, the fabulous creature had two immense, curving, teardrop-shaped protuberances of faceted jet.

Its long, tapering, and cylindrical body was plated with overlapping flat rings of flashing silver, powdered with dust of azure. Like the goblin steed of some impossible elf-knight, it flashed through the dim amber gloom on its undreamable mission!

Then my dazzlement woke to astonished awe—for I glimpsed tasseled, silken reins affixed to the base of the delicate antennae—a saddle of padded and sumptuous velvet belted about the torpedo-like torso of the winged creature—and seated therein—an elfin knight in truth!

Graceful—slim as a ballet dancer—feminine in his delicate beauty—the chevalier mounted upon this airy courser was all but nude. A cuirass of gilt leather formed a broad flat collar about his slim throat and shielded his hairless, girlish chest, tapering to join the girdle he wore low about his hips. Gems flashed and winked in the gilt leather—red, green, and indigo.

This elfin chevalier wore a strange, complicated helm of glittering glass: the design was vaguely like that of antique Japanese armor. A long gauzy plume of gossamer white floated back from the horns of this fantastical helm.

Beneath the helm, this face was elfin in its delicate beauty—large amber-golden eyes set aslant in a fine-boned, heart-shaped, point-chinned face. His skin was the mellow tone of old ivory and his mouth a dainty pink rosebud.

His shoulders and arms were bare, as were his long graceful legs, but he wore stiff brocade gauntlets, heavy with gold wire and flashing purple stones, and high swash-topped corsair boots of scarlet leather, with high gilt heels and jeweled buckles.

A long cloth of purple was wound about his supple loins, and attached to his warrior-harness he wore a long rapier like a curved glass needle.

As I hung in mid-air, stunned with amazement at this gorgeous vision, the glittering elf-knight on his dragonfly-steed flashed by me in a twinkling and was gone.

But in his track came yet another, this one cloaked in drifting veils of misty gray, his loincloth of deep blue, his helm of intricate and diamond-studded silver, his plume a wisp of shimmering gold.

The second rider bore a slim lance of sharp glass, from which a long banderole of su!phurous yellow, charged with a nine-pointed star of deep black, slowly uncoiled behind him in his flight.

He too flashed past me, and now I saw that the two elfin warriors were ascending to a higher level—perhaps to the immensely broad branch far above me.

They were the fore guard of a stately train, for now came three in blazing yellow surcoats, the black star on their breasts, their slim-featured faces masked behind visors of silver cloth, riding abreast like an honor guard.

And behind them, borne through the misty golden twilight like Titania in her chariot, came a delicate car of fluted pearl shaped like a scallop shell, drawn by four gigantic dragonflies. Throned therein on many-colored pillows was a man in a long narrow robe of fierce yellow with a spiky crown of black crystals on his brows and fathomless eyes of emerald flame, cold and intelligent and subtle. In his ungauntleted hand he bore a scepter like a rod of black crystal.

This aerial entourage ascended to the vast branch above me, and, drawn by a fascination I cannot describe, I floated on their heels—to a vision of supernal beauty transcending description.

For atop the broad level branch ran a great boulevard of gray stone. And half a mile away, where the bough met and joined with the colossal trunk of the forest giant, a city built of ten thousand jewels flashed and glittered in the crotch of the tremendous tree!

Thus I first looked upon the gemmy ramparts of Phaolon the Glorious—Jewel City of the Goddess-Queen—capital of the airy kingdom of the Laonese—wherein I was to find my heart, my destiny, and my own peculiar doom!

As one enmeshed in dream I followed the flying entourage to the landing place before the high-turreted gates of the Jewel City.

Their dragonfly steeds drifted to a landing, as did the team which drew the pearly chariot of the man in yellow robes who wore the spiky miter of flashing black crystals.

A party of fairy knights came forth to greet them with high ceremony. Elfin heralds in jeweled tabards like glittering tapestries flourished long, fluted silvery horns. An honor guard in colors of gold and emerald saluted stiffly and led the way through gates that blazed with turquoise and topaz ... and I followed after, bedazzled by such beauty.

Into the faerie metropolis the party of visitors swept, and up a tall narrow staircase of shimmering crystals toward a towered edifice, like Queen Mab's palace.

Drawn up to either side, the elfin populace watched, but with no cheering. Mute and sullen and unhappy were their expressions, or fiercely resentful, or tragic and bitter. It was as if a cruel and conquering emperor had arrived at their gates to demand utter surrender.

Into the mosque-domed palace they swept with regal and imperious stride. Through a tall, Gothic-pointed gateway studded with immense, glittering jewels they swaggered, the gaunt, cold-eyed man with the crown of spiky black crystals striding before them with the proud stance of a conqueror. And at their heels, unseen, I flitted like an invisible spirit attendant on the presence of some master sorcerer.

The visiting party at length entered a vast, domed audience hall, floored with milky jade and roofed with a vaulted dome of lucent ruby through which struck level shafts of burning and sanguine splendor.

Here was assembled a princely company, begowned and begemmed in fantastic panoply—the court of some Princess of Faerie—the Hall of a Goblin Queen! They stood

T. KIRK

silent, with closed faces, bending inscrutable gaze on the tall man in narrow robes of fierce, incandescent yellow, who strode through the throng, glancing neither to right nor left, bearing himself with all the arrogance of an emperor.

They neither bowed nor made any salute as he passed, and their elfin features were impassive and unreadable; but I saw anguish in the eyes of the women, and despair was written on many a brow. Intrigued by the mystery, by the strange and pregnant drama of the scene upon which I had intruded, I lingered a time to see what would occur.

In the midst of the immensity of the ruby-domed hall a slim throne towered atop a pedestal of sparkling crystal. The chair, with its curved and slender legs of gilt, and high, fluted back, resembled for all the world a chair from the reign of Louis XIV.

The throne stood empty; slim-legged heralds, resting the belled mouths of long silver bugles on their hips, stood in a semicircle about the untenanted throne, gems twinkling on their tabards. A bald, fat-paunched chamberlain in thick robes of imperial purple strode from the throng to bow stiffly before the cruel-faced man in the narrow yellow robes.

There ensued a lengthy pause in which I sensed, but could not hear, the taut-stretched, aching silence.

And then the bugles blew!

As a field of gorgeous flowers bows beneath a wave of wind, all that splendid and glittering company sank in profound obeisance before the young woman who appeared in a tall, pointed doorway. She swept through the kneeling throng, past the tall, cold-faced man crowned with black crystals, mounted the several tall steps of the dais, and seated herself in the gold throne.

And for the first time I looked upon the incredible, the heart-shaking beauty of Niamh—Niamh of Phaolon, Goddess-Queen of the Jewel City!

Niamh—the Queen of the Green Star! And queen of my heart from that first, breathless moment to the last moment of my life!

Chapter 4

PRINCESS OF THE JEWEL CITY

How can I describe her as I first saw her, enthroned in her golden chair under that immense dome of dim and luminous ruby? Words, I think, fail and falter before the task of describing such utter perfection of feminine beauty.

She was young, a girl, a mere child: she looked perhaps fourteen when I saw her first in the Great Hall of Phaolon. Slim and graceful as a dancing girl, with her slight, tip-tilted breasts and long, slender legs, she had the coltish grace of an adolescent which contrasted with her regal, queenly dignity.

She wore robes of dull, heavy plush—plush with a shimmering silvery nap—plush the dim hue of damask roses. A scooping neckline exposed the upper slopes of her shallow, adolescent breasts, laid bare her slim shoulders and the fragility of her slender throat. All of her upper bosom was the creamy hue of old mellow ivory.

The bodice of her gown fitted her like a second skin, and clung seductively to the slender waist and smooth, boyish hips of Niamh. But from her girdle, slung low about her hips in the style of the Renaissance, the rose plush skirts of the gown swelled out like the open petals of some soft, lovely flower. This gown was slit up the sides, demurely revealing the silken loveliness of her soft, smooth long legs, naked to the upper thigh, and from beneath the hem of this gown could be glimpsed the tiny, exquisite foot of a Mandarin princess, shod in slippers of golden filigree.

From heavy, belling puffed sleeves, her slim arms ex-

tended, bare and unadorned. In all that splendid company,
Niamh alone wore no gems at breast or throat, lobe or
brow or fingers. She had no need of the frozen mineral
fire to add luster or brilliance to her loveliness.

Her face was fine-boned, heart-shaped, exquisite.
Beneath delicately arched brows, her eyes were enormous
wells of depthless amber flame wherein flakes of gold fire
trembled. Thick jetty lashes enshadowed the dark flame of
her eyes, but her hair, elaborately teased and twisted and
coiffed, was startlingly white: a fantastic confection of
frosted sugar, an exquisite construction of spun silver.

Her mouth was a luscious rosebud, daintily pink, moist-
ly seductive.

A delicate flower of superb and breathtaking loveliness
was Niamh the Fair, when first I looked upon her there
on the gilt throne, bathed in shafts of somber and ruby
light from the hollow dome above.

The portly chamberlain rang his great silver mace of
office against the polished tiles; and there commenced a
scene of dramatic confrontation which baffled and maddened me—for, not only was it conducted in a language
unknown to me, but a language whose tones I could not
even hear!

The spirit-state in which I floated unseen had annoying
properties. Although I could see clearly, by the agency of
some interaction of forces inexplicable to me then and
now, no sound whatsoever reached my impalpable senses.
Thus it was that the tense drama now enacted before me
was conducted in total silence, insofar as I was concerned.

The tall gaunt man with the cruel face and intense eyes,
whose name was Akhmim, as I later learned, seemed to
be presenting the princess with an ultimatum of some sort.
He set forth his terms with vehement gestures and em-
phatic curtness, dictating, as I gathered, from a position of
superiority. That his terms were unpalatable I assumed
from the glum expressions on the faces of those courtiers
nearest to me; and that they were peremptory and affron-
tive I gathered from the stiffness of Niamh's posture and
from the rich color that glowed in her cheeks.

There was a sneering insolence in Akhmim's arrogant
posture, in the negligent courtesy he made to the throne,
and in the insufferable smugness wherewith he rested his

case, awaiting with folded arms and lofty expression the reply of the princess.

As for Niamh, long lashes hooded the amber fire of her eyes, but indignation colored her cheeks and her breasts rose and fell, panting with suppressed fury.

As for me, although I understood none of this, I longed to seize Akhmim by the scruff of the neck and the seat of his robe and chuck him out of the hall in a most unceremonious manner, calculated to bruise his self-importance, if not even more tender portions of his physical anatomy. And if I read correctly the outrage and insult that smoldered in the gaze of many of Niamh's courtiers, there were many in the hall that day who would have applauded such an act, had it been possible for me to perform it.

Still Niamh hesitated before giving her answer to the ultimatum of Akhmim. I somehow sensed that her reply, once given, would be irrevocable.

Then something caught my attention, and drew me from this scene of tension. Niamh's gilt throne rose on a many-tiered pedestal in the center of the hall; but the hall itself was cruciform, like the crux formed by the two passages of a cathedral, and, where the nave of a cathedral would be, there rose a most curious structure. It was like an immense sarcophagus, but one built of delicate blown glass, chased with arabesques and painted with inscriptions in a tongue unknown to me.

Within this crystal coffin there reposed the body of a man so perfectly preserved that his appearance was in all details utterly lifelike. Indeed, you would have unhesitatingly sworn he was not dead at all, but lay in light slumber. The bloom of life was on his cheeks, his grim lips were moist, almost you saw his deep chest tremble to the susurration of light breathing.

In no way did he resemble the dainty, effeminate men of Phaolon. Where they were small and exquisite, he was tall, broad of shoulder, with great arms and thighs of mighty girth. Where their limbs were delicate as those of smooth young girls, his were corded with sinews, thick with swelling thews. Where their faces were fine-boned and elfin, his was a rude frame of jutting bone, square and massive of jaw, swarthy of hue, and, lacking their smoothness, rough and harsh as from the burning kiss of tropic suns and the lash of stinging tempests.

He had been a mighty warrior, I guessed, and perhaps

had led many a war-host in the field: for the stern, grim-lipped air of command lay about him like a crimson cloak.

He was unclothed, the Sleeping One—which, as I later learned, was what the folk of Phaolon called the warrior in the crystal coffin—and his great arms lay folded upon his breast, where they were clenched about the massive pommel of a gigantic broadsword of blue steel. A glittering scarlet crystal flashed and winked in the pommel of that sword.

Something about the Sleeping One caught my attention, drew me to the glass sarcophagus wherein he lay enshrined. I cannot explain the fascination that mighty form exerted upon my imagination; it was as if every line and lineament of those grim features was engraved upon the tablets of my memory—as if I had known him, somewhere, somewhen, perhaps in some former life. ...

I drifted down toward the great figure, where it lay stretched out upon a pallet of sumptuous velvets. And then there occurred a miracle, the strangest among the many I had thus far experienced; for my spirit-self floated down to scrutinize the body of the Sleeping One—and *entered it*—

And lived again in human flesh!

The transition from disembodied spirit to a spirit which dwelt in living flesh was instantaneous and utterly astounding. In my spirit-state I had been aware of no bodily sensations whatsoever—now the pulse thundered in my temples, the heart labored in my breast, and my lungs ached, starving for air!

With an involuntary start of surprise, my thews convulsed; I rose from my pallet, brandishing my arms, and the great broadsword to which I clung clove through the glass sarcophagus, shattering it to ten thousand ringing shards!

The explosion of shattering glass filled the hall with ringing echoes. A hundred startled eyes turned to see me rise from my place among the glorious dead. The miracle of my resurrection wrung a gasp of stupefied amazement from a hundred throats.

But none in all that place were more astounded at this turn of events than was I myself!

For I had not willed myself down into that dead or

sleeping form. Hovering near, I had been caught helpless in the attraction of some force unknown to me, sucked down as by a vortex into that body, helpless to resist the suction as any chip caught in a maelstrom.

Niamh stared at me with unbelief in her wide eyes and astonishment written in her face.

From where he stood before the throne, Akhmim regarded me as if I were an apparition. I sensed that something in my resurrection—perhaps its timing, which had come almost as if in answer to his ultimatum—disconcerted him, shook his arrogance, struck doubt into the armor of his confidence.

For a breathless moment he stood, twisted about awkwardly in his stiff robes, looking uncomfortable and somehow foolish. And he knew it, for he paled and bit his lip and tugged at his garments as if to rearrange them.

For a long moment the entire company stood frozen in shock. No one spoke or moved. Then, from among a rank of courtiers who stood in a semicircle behind Niamh's throne, one elderly sage thrust himself to the fore and addressed me. From the rising lilt of his tones I gathered it was an interrogation. The only trouble was that the question was spoken in a language completely unknown to me—a fluid, musical tongue that sounded rather like a cross between Hawaiian and French, with a sibilant tang of old Castilian.

The question thus addressed to me was spoken in loud, clear tones fully audible to all who stood within the ruby-domed hall. Whatever the nature of the query may have been, I sensed from the breathless silence that followed upon the old man's words, and from the keen and alert fixity with which all eyes were trained upon me, that it was one of enormous importance. Without exception, all who stood there waited in tense expectancy for my reply.

From the moment I had stood up, shattering free of the glass sarcophagus, I had stood motionlessly, my face impassive, clenching the mighty broadsword in one scarred fist. I had not chosen this immobile stance consciously—the fact of the matter was that I was suffering exquisitely from the torment of renewed circulation. How long this trance-bound body had slept in its transparent tomb I did not know, but the pins-and-needles sensation of numb flesh awakening and the intolerable ache of long-unused muscles forced to work again, combined in a torture beyond description.

In my agony, I scarcely heard the sage's query, and it was not until long after that I realized its importance, and the import of my answer. By pure accident, without even thinking, I did precisely the right thing.

I—*nodded*.

And in the next instant the ruby dome above rang to a peal of thunderous acclamation. Joy blazed in the eyes of the throng; exaltation shone in their happy faces. Indescribable relief and bliss glowed in the face of Niamh the Fair. Her eyes shone down on me, brilliant with an inexplicable fervor, and she clasped her small hands to her throbbing heart in an ecstasy beyond all my comprehension.

A burly, hard-faced guard captain, who stood very near the foot of his princess' dais, turned upon me a gaze of wordless adoration. Then he removed his sword from his scabbard and raised it aloft in salute to me.

A hundred swords leaped from their scabbards to flash aloft like narrow mirrors in the rich glory from above.

And from a hundred throats rang one word—

"Chong! *Chong!* CHONG!"

And I knew it was no word, but a name.

My name!

Chapter 5

THE WISDOM OF KHIN-NOM

At the command of my royal hostess, a gorgeously-appointed suite of apartments was reserved for me, and a squadron of guards-warriors vied for the honor of serving me, led by the hard-faced captain who had been the first of all to hail me. His name was Panthon.

My own name I first mistook to be Kyr-Chong, for thus I was addressed by all who spoke to me, including Panthon and his warriors. It was only later, as I became familiar with the oddly musical language spoken by the Laonese, as the folk of Phaolon term their race, that I came to understand the phoneme *kyr* was a prefix of honor, denoting something like "Lord Chong" or perhaps "Sir Chong"; as for "Chong" itself, it was an affectionate diminutive, used in a blending of respect and love, as the Englishmen of old referred to Richard the Lionhearted as "stout old Rick" or as those of a later age spoke of Henry V as "Hal" or "Harry."

My full name, it seemed, was Chongaphon tai-Vena-Vena, and the allusions above to the Lionheart and the victor of Agincourt are not far off the mark. For Lord Chong had been a warrior hero of mythic fame, a doer of legendary deeds. No doubt existed in those who clustered about me on my rare public appearances but that I was that mighty man, reborn again in my original body, which had been perfectly preserved against just such an eventuality. An ancient prophecy had been made that someday in great time of need I would return again to lead the warriors of Phaolon the Jewel City to victories and triumphs

31

as of old, and to save the realm from doom in its hour of ultimate peril.

I am certain that my total ignorance of the Laonese, of their history, their language, and their ways, was carefully kept secret from the courtiers and the commonfolk. The most embarrassing element in my "amnesia"—for thus it was regarded—was my lack of any familiarity with the language. This was first on the agenda of my education.

My tutor in all things was the same elderly sage who had addressed me across the frozen throng on the day of my revivification. His name was Khin-nom and he was one of the chief advisors of the princess. I am at a loss to find an office relative to his in terms of Terrene history. It is not that he was premier or prime minister or secretary of state or a politician of any kind, such offices being thoroughly unknown among the Laonese, who place all authority and power in the hands of the monarch alone. He was simply a man of great age and wit and learning, with experience in every field of knowledge: call him a philosopher and you will not be far from the truth.

Khin-nom treated me with the utmost deference during our linguistic sessions, but he was too shrewd, too intelligent, to regard me with the awe and veneration others displayed toward me, which amounted virtually to worship. For several hours each day he practiced with me in the Laonese tongue, and his method of teaching was strikingly practical. The first such session opened with him calling my attention to his lifted forefinger; he pronounced in clear tones the word *phos*, which I repeated aloud, immediately catching onto the idea that this was to be a language lesson.

Next he opened the fingers of his closed fist one by one, and spoke the word *phosa*, which I assumed correctly to be the plural. Then, indicating his entire hand, he pronounced the word *ephosa*; he then gave me the Laonese words for the wrist, forearm, elbow, shoulder, neck, chin, and so on, indicating each bodily part and speaking the relevant Laonese word in clear enunciation. That first session lasted all of one afternoon, and once I had been introduced to a dozen or fifteen words in this manner, we relaxed and he refreshed me on what I had learned by pointing to random parts of his anatomy and eliciting from me its name in Laonese. I made few errors.

Thereafter we met every day, immediately following the

noon meal. Each subsequent lesson opened with a quick review of what I had learned in the last, before continuing on to a fresh group of words. These early sessions were quite easy. Parts of the body, colors, garments, the names of substances like stone, wood, crystal, and metal, these I mastered with surprising ease, almost as if I were merely remembering a language I had once known, rather than attempting to learn a new one. The sessions gradually became much more difficult, as we passed beyond physical objects into abstractions such as verbs, adverbs, and adjectives.

I have always had a knack for languages, and in my youth had taught myself, or had learned from private tutors, not only German, Latin, and a sketchy familiarity with Tibetan and Hebrew, but also Greek and Sanskrit. However, I had never before had any reason to master a language so quickly, and without already sharing a common tongue with the man who was teaching me; so my Laonese lessons were simultaneously easier and more difficult than my previous linguistic studies, if you see what I mean.

However, working steadily away at it for hours at a time, day after day, I learned the language in what seems a remarkably short time—enough of it to be able to handle myself in casual conversation, at least. My tutor seemed quite satisfied with the progress I was making, and I was quite impressed with it myself.

This Khin-nom was a dignified, aristocratic man of elderly years. He looked about sixty, but actually this is only a guess on my part and I have no idea as to his precise age, for among the Laonese it is considered poor manners to inquire into the subject, which is taboo with them for some reason I never learned.

He was rather tall for his race, three or four inches under six feet, and of slender build, with long beautiful hands, expressive eyes, and a lean, bony face the color of old parchment. I believe he was bald, as is commonly the case among those of the Laonese who attain to a dignified old age, but as he habitually wore a tall, five-sided hat of stiff brocade, I cannot be certain. He had a long, pointed chin which was adorned by a narrow beard he kept dyed in prismatic colors to match the high-necked, long-sleeved robes he wore. The colors he favored were generally indigo, rust, chartreuse, and a virulent shade of green.

I have said that Khin-nom approached the task of instructing me in the Laonese tongue in a practical manner. By this I mean that we plunged at once into our language lessons and did not deviate from them into other areas of discussion. Every afternoon he appeared in my suite, bowed gracefully with both hands pressed together, seated himself on a stool of carved ivory, and proceeded at once with the lessons. Later on, as I became steadily more proficient in the Laonese tongue, I attempted to make halting conversation with him several times, in order to learn the answers to some of the many questions which tormented my curiosity. But to each of these conversational overtures he gracefully declined comment. I assumed that either he had been ordered to answer none of my questions, or that he preferred not to for reasons of his own.

As I gradually became able to understand the language and to make myself understood in it, however, I sought answers to some of the mysteries that plagued me from the warriors who attended me, principally from grizzled Panthon.

He was a stern-faced soldier of about forty, his thin hair cut short and grizzled at the temples, his bearing stiff and martial, and there was about him none of the daintiness or languor which lent most of the male Laonese, regardless of age, a certain elfin effeminacy.

"Panthon," I would ask him, when we were alone, "who do your people think me to be?"

"Chong the Mighty come again, lord," he would reply gruffly.

"Is it a precept of your religion that the dead are reborn and live again?"

The question seemed to baffle him, and he fumbled for a reply. I eventually gathered that my case was without precedent and that the Laonese religion had no especial teaching on the matter of rebirth: but, as it was self-evident that I was Chong the Mighty, and as my rebirth had been witnessed by the entire court, the fact of it was obvious.

"Does it not puzzle those who think me Chong the Mighty returned to life, that I need to be taught your language all over again, that I need to be instructed in

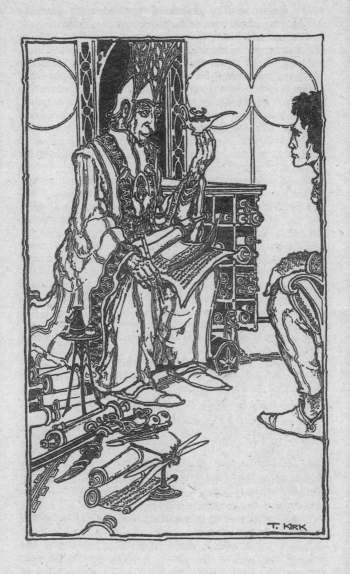

your language as if I had never before known it?" I asked.

Again he did not seem to know how to answer me. A simple man of few words, my honest, faithful Panthon, and not very much given to thinking things out on his own. I gathered from his halting reply that my seclusion kept very many from knowing that I had to be taught the language; and, anyway, I was Chong. If Chong wished to be taught something, who could question it? My reasons, doubtless, were my own: and that was that.

Simple, loyal Panthon!

Once in a while, on formal occasions, I dined in state before the assembled court and in the company of the exquisite young princess, in the grand banquet hall of her palace.

These feasts were ceremonial functions, performed periodically, to which members of the various ranks of the aristocracies were invited on a sort of rotation system. The Laonese culture was very ancient and had been stable for millennia, until by now it had become so encrusted with tradition that formalities and precedents governed every detail of dress and deportment, every facet of daily life. Such banquets, stiff with punctilio, elaborately ceremonious to the point of boredom, were virtually unendurable. But en route to one of them, accompanied by the sage Khin-nom, I encountered something which moved me deeply.

We had descended a coiling staircase of carven alabaster and were about to enter a long, high-roofed corridor lined with an honor guard of bejeweled and beplumed Laonese chivalry, when I stopped short, my gaze caught by a most imposing monument.

There was a huge rotunda at the base of this spiral stairway from which the corridor branched off, and rising from the exact center of this rotunda was a colossal statue of a heroic youth shielding his breast with an arrow-studded buckler, lifting his face defiantly to heaven, thrusting skyward with the hilt of a broken sword.

The substance from which some Laonese Michelangelo or Canova had carved this heroic colossus was a sparkling crystal which resembled diamond in its purity and multi-colored fire, but which was in fact, as I later learned, organic. The crystalline substance, however, was enormously rare and valuable, in that respect also not unlike diamond.

And the statue was thirty feet high!

I stared up at it in amazement, struck not only by the fabulous richness of the thing, but by the brilliance of its artistic genius.

As I paused, old Khin-nom halted, and eyed me shrewdly and with a touch of humor in the sly expression of his eyes as I stood gaping.

"Does my lord recognize the figure?" he purred.

I admitted that I did not—which must have amused the wise old philosopher, although he was too clever to show it.

"It is yourself, my lord, in the fourteenth of your Deeds, the time you battled against and slew the Great Ythid of Diompharna," he said casually.

I knew enough of the language of this strange, mist-veiled world of the Green Star by now to recognize the word. To the Laonese, the *ythid* is a monster so dread as to have become symbolic and mythological, save that such reptiles, though rare, do indeed exist.

We walked on in silence. As for myself, I was somewhat shaken. It is, after all, not every day that a man finds out he is a dragon slayer!

I began to entertain doubts as to the wisdom of continuing my imposture of a legendary hero miraculously returned to life. It is all very well to be the reincarnation of a famous dragon killer of yore, but what if my royal hostess suddenly called upon me to repeat my celebrated deed?

Part II

THE BOOK OF NIAMH
THE FAIR

Chapter 6

THE SHADOW OF AKHMIM

The banquet to which we were bound on that particular evening was one of the frequent ceremonial functions tradition required of the Jewel City monarch.

The life of the princess was bound to every side by centuries-old patterns of enormously complicated tradition and ritual. Periodically, the Princess of Phaolon was required to feast representatives of the several aristocracies of her realm; I have no idea as to the reason why. It may have been something in the nature of a renewal of the aristocrats in their rank, or a symbolic token of the interdependency of the sovereign and the aristocracies, ritualized by their sharing of a common meal, or something to do with the national religion, which as yet I understood imperfectly.

At any rate, such occasions were a crashing bore, interminable evening-long meals of thirty or forty courses, interspersed with flowery speeches, ceremonial dances and poetry recitals, elaborate courtesies, and obscure traditional gestures, such as the pouring of three drops from every winecup into silver salvers borne around the banquet hall by an endless succession of pages, for no conceivable reason or purpose.

Certain different incenses were burned during certain courses by Laonese priests in elaborately different robes and accouterments stationed at small altars situated here and there. Something like spruce gum was burned during a course of small cubes of beef-like meat in cream sauce, skewered with tiny silver forks; a thickly odorous incense like myrrh was sizzled in golden pans during a course of breaded fish; a sharp and pungent perfume, like pine needles, was poured on braziers of coals during yet another course consisting of small slivers of sweet white meat cooked in sugary wine.

The elaborately artificial aspects of these interminable banquets was unendurable. Nobody knew why or how these customs had arisen, but arisen they had, and, once hallowed by a few centuries of tradition, a facet of behavior became crystallized in Laonese society and was there to stay.

Luckily for me, during the early phases of my education when I was still largely unfamiliar with the language, no one required me to deliver any of the lengthy speeches, flowery compliments, or recitals of national poetry, which droned on more or less constantly during the succession of courses. I was politely ignored during these banquets, for it was thought that a ritual period of acclimatization was required of one who had but recently returned from the World Above, as the Laonese conception of heaven is termed. So I just nibbled at the various courses, guzzled wine, and tried to ignore the so-called festivities.

Custom, ritual, precedent, and tradition rule the Laonese aristocracies and, to a lesser extent, the common folk, and this endlessly complicated code of ceremonial behavior controlled and governed virtually every phase and detail of everyday life. In this, as in certain other things, it resembled the Chinese civilization of the imperial periods.

I use the plural, "aristocracies," because the Laonese society was an hierarchical one, made up of a number of different ranks. There were, for example, what might be called the landed gentry—members of ancient families with an hereditary claim to certain territories of the realm. Members of this aristocracy were known as the *thurkūz*. Their highest ranking member and most vocal spokesman was a stiff-necked old woman, the Kyra Vaonica du Kaikoos, which translates as Lady (or Dame) Vaonica of Kaikoos; she was a sort of duchess.

The second aristocracy was made up of those families descended from Laonese patriots or heroes who had been ennobled for their services to the throne, just as English monarchs have bestowed titles on their war heroes like Lord Nelson or the Duke of Wellington. The custom of honoring outstanding heroes with ranks and titles was popular among earlier Laonese sovereigns, but had died out somewhat lately. However, these honors were of a different kind and nature from those of the *thurkūz*, the landed gentry. This second aristocracy was called the *aophet*, which means something like "sprung from the heroes." In my incarnation as Lord Chong, I belonged to this particular aristocracy myself. In fact, I now took precedence as highest ranking peer and spokesman of the *aophet*, displacing a suave baron named Iohom who had been senior lord of the *aophet* before my revivification.

There was a third aristocracy whose differences from the others was a subtle one, so subtle I never quite managed to grasp the difference. It consisted of those with titular honors, some exceedingly fanciful, others thoroughly devoid of meaning as far as I could see. This particular aristocracy, the *iophua*, held hereditary honors such as Lord Custodian of the Nine Ivory Batons, or Privy Guardian of the Silver Book of Hshan, or High Steward of the Scarlet Flask, and so on.

A tradition-encrusted people, the Laonese! For never once did I see the Lord Custodian with a baton of any kind, much less an ivory one. The High Steward had a noticeable fondness for the wine flask, all right, but I never saw him with a scarlet one. And as for the Privy Guardian, from the way he usually snored through the poetry recitals, I cannot conceive of him as possessing interest in any book, much less Hshan's.

There was one thing that could be said for these formal banquets, and that was that they gave me a chance to see Niamh.

At these functions, the Laonese dine from low taborets while seated cross-legged on cushions. But the princess and I, as only befitting our superior degree, sat in regular chairs at opposite ends of a dais. I thus had the pleasant opportunity to feast my eyes on her while feasting my belly.

How lovely she was! Sapling-slim, demure, exquisite as a fairy princess. I have had little to do with women; during my life on Earth, as a cripple, it seemed to me impossible that I could ever be anything other than an object of either pity or contempt in the eyes of a beautiful woman. Desiring to be neither, I avoided their company, although my appetite was as normal as that of any whole and healthy man. Now I basked in the bliss of her nearness, and the shy sidewise looks she sometimes cast at me, demurely, from under silken lashes, did not escape me. How wondrous strange it was, to feel myself the object of a beautiful girl's admiration! How thrilling to know myself tall and strong, a hero, a warrior of immortal deeds, in the eyes of all who looked upon me!

At times I questioned my wisdom in lingering here on the World of the Green Star. I was not the mythic Hercules they fancied me to be, but a strange wanderer come hence on a weird voyage, caught in a body that was not my own, enjoying the worship and adulation which belonged to someone else. I feel certain that the old sage, Khin-nom, doubted the truth of my revivification. Suppose questions were asked of me concerning my first life as Lord Chong—questions I could not answer, bearing on a life that I had never lived? Would it not be wiser for me to quit this borrowed body and return to take up the life that was my own?

I hesitated—I lingered—I procrastinated; and can any wonder that I put off returning to the body of a cripple, turning my back on this weird and gorgeous world of mile-high trees, jewelbox cities, and elfin knights mounted on dragonflies? For what was there for me to go home to, but a dreary life of books and dreams, prisoned in a paralyzed carcass that could not take a step without assistance?

And so I stayed on ... and lost my heart.

Time and again I puzzled over the meaning of that dramatic scene I had interrupted with my involuntary resurrection. What was the substance of that tense confrontation I had spied upon unseen, when the cold-faced man in robes of eye-hurting yellow, crowned with spiky black crystals, had stood in challenge before the tall throne of Phaolon and hurled his insolence in the flower-like face of Niamh the Fair?

The elderly philosopher but tugged at his indigo beard, avoiding my questions by ignoring them and pressing on with our unremitting language lessons. Captain Panthon, usually my prime source of information, seemed oddly reluctant to reply to my queries. I have since concluded that his reluctance was in deference to hallowed tradition: men of the *khaweng-ya*, the warrior class, do not discuss high matters; the doings of their lords and betters are subjects unfit for gossip or speculation.

Bit by bit I pieced together a patchwork picture of the situation, gathering hints and clues from a careless word let fall in my presence, a scrap of conversation overheard, or veiled references murmured when I was not supposed to be listening.

The man in the yellow robes, it seemed, had been Akhmim, who was the prince of another tree-city called Ardha. His ultimatum was a marriage proposal!

It seems that precedent and tradition hallow the masculine gender, alone deemed fit to wield sovereignty. A Queen regnant is a novelty unheard-of in all the placid millennia of Laonese annals. It is not exactly that a woman ruler is forbidden by any law of gods or men: it is simply something new and strange and different. And to the timid, ephemeral Laonese, whose lives are dominated by ritual and antique custom, the new and novel is anathema, or at least highly suspect.

Niamh was a slave to custom, too; but it is the art of a monarch to interpret tradition in support of the royal will. And the will of princes is less subject to the ghostly authority of the past than are the wills of those who are accustomed to being ruled over by princes.

For ages a tension has stretched between the two tree-cities. Nothing so overt as war—that custom happily is most rare here on the World of the Green Star—but a certain rivalry, an unease. The folk of Phaolon, then, were on the horns of a particularly galling dilemma. On the one

hand, every precept of custom and tradition cried out that
a princess could not rule alone; on the other, they loathed
the notion of yielding the hand of their beloved Niamh to
the unwelcome and unloved Tyrant-Prince of Ardha.

Niamh had weighed the custom of masculine rule
against the traditional envy and suspicion the folk of
Phaolon felt for the men of Ardha, and had chosen the
course of action least offensive to tradition—she would
rule alone.

On the day of my resurrection, Akhmim of Ardha had
come with an ultimatum. The benign will of the World
Above, the unanimous precedent of a thousand regnant
kings, the crushing weight of age-old authority, demanded
she wed a prince of her rank and yield primacy to him.
Only the shadowy divinities of the World Above knew
what shattering thunderbolts of calamity and cataclysm
would ensue, if a woman maintained her grasp on the
throne of Phaolon in blind defiance of tradition and holy
precedent. Did the Princess Niamh, in her mad arrogance
and folly, possess some secret sign from heaven that the
World Above would tolerate her mad ambition? Akhmim
cried aloud to the Green Star for some token or omen
that heaven favored her in her folly—

*And in that fateful moment, I thundered to life in my
tomb!*

Small wonder that at the time I sensed my coming forth
had disconcerted Akhmim, throwing him off-balance.
"Off-balance" indeed! He had been petrified with horror,
frozen with unbelieving shock. What sign could have been
more dramatic than my springing to life, the shards of my
splintered sarcophagus ringing about me on the glistening
pave?

None could blame the Princess of Phaolon for interpret-
ing my miraculous return to the lands of the living as a
sign from the World Above. The timing of the event alone
confirmed it. A more sensationally dramatic affirmation of
Niamh's sacred right to her throne could hardly have been
imagined than the sudden reincarnation of the mighty
Chong, hero of a thousand legends, the mythic defender
of her own great dynasty in the age of her forefathers.

Akhmim, crushed, shaken to the core, had fled the hall
in confusion, and no word had come from him since.

But his shadow lay over the Jewel City like a grim pall,
like a cold gloom of ominous fate to come. So close had

Akhmim stood to the throne he coveted, so swift had fate snatched it from his grasp, that few could doubt he would not seek again to fulfill his desires.

And in his path, I stood alone!

Chapter 7

THE DANCE OF THE ZAIPH

The time came when I had mastered the lovely, musical language of the Laonese.

To tell the truth, the ease and rapidity with which I had learned the tongue of this strange world surprised me. It even frightened me a little.

It was not so much like learning a new language—a dreary process of word drills and memorizing—as it was like *remembering* a language I had known long, long ago, and all but forgotten with the years.

Could there be any truth to the Laonese belief that I was their mighty hero of old come again? Who was this Kyr Chong the Mighty—how was it that his body had been so perfectly preserved that when I, a wandering spirit, had chanced to wander near, it could be reanimated to live again?

One pleasant result of mastering the tongue was that, now my lessons were done, the old sage Khin-nom permitted himself to be engaged in conversation. The wily old philosopher even granted me the answers to a few questions.

He smiled slyly, and replied to my query in his soft, purring voice: "Surely my lord recalls that he did not ever die, but fell victim to the wizard's spell!"

"I remember nothing of my former life, Khin-nom; you who have had to patiently teach me the tongue all over again must surely know that! I suspect death must be as shattering a trauma as birth, and spirits thrust forth suddenly on the dark wind disperse, their memories wiped

46

clean by the cataclysmic experience ... but what do you mean, I never died? *What* wizard—and *what* spell?"

We were in the sage's own suite, that day. A cool, pleasant, empty room of whitewashed walls, and many windows open to a murmuring infinity of leafy solitude. A room filled to the brim with peace and calm; a room for contemplation.

From a rack of scrolls he plucked one heavy tube of parchment. Minute rows of hooked characters marched up and down the sheet when he unfolded it, and his narrow finger followed them up and down, down and up—the Laonese script is written boustrophedon, like Hittite: back and forth, as an ox plows a field.

He chanted some poetry at me, but I understood little of it. The bardic epics that form the center of Phaolon's national literature, the so-called Eight Classics, are written in an obscure, highfalutin diction very unlike everyday speech.

"What is that, Khin-nom?" I asked impatiently.

He hooded his eyes, voice suave. "The epic of your Thirty Deeds, my lord! The thirtieth and last was to rid the world of that wizard called *Kryaphaom*, the Lord of Ghosts. 'Twas he who sundered your spirit from your flesh and hurled it forth into the void of mists beyond the world, beyond the Green Star itself. You struck him down to death in that same moment, but already the death-like sleep of a thousand years was upon you. Our sacred forefathers mourned you, and preserved your flesh in pure crystal against the time ordained, when your spirit should come wandering home from beyond the stars . . ."

My skin crawled at the sly whisper, and my nape hairs prickled in primal awe. His account was uncanny in its closeness to the facts—for my spirit had in truth come to this world from beyond the stars. From the dim twilight of elder Mars the flickering beacon of the Green Star had called to me with a strange fascination ... *could it be that I remembered it from another life?*

Could it be that I really was Chong, or had once been him, many lives before this last? Did the eternal human spirit travel an endless cycle of birth and death and rebirth, as the Buddhists taught and the lamas of Tibet believed? But if so, why was it that I remembered nothing of my former life as Chong the Mighty, hero of Phaolon and ancient defender of its age-old throne?

Do the memories of one life fade, under the accumulation of experiences, as life upon life is laid upon the soul like a palimpsest?

The implications of this suggestion were soul-shaking, world-changing: I set them from me firmly, changing the subject.

"How do you, who dwell under eternal mists, know anything of the stars?" I demanded.

"There are rifts in the clouds that veil us from heaven," he said slyly. "In the same wise, there may come rifts in the forgetfulness that clouds my lord's mind, and gleams of memory from his life as Chong may shine through...."

An even more pleasant result of my mastery of the language was that now I saw much more of the exquisite princess.

And not just at those endless formal banquets which I have described, either; we had several meetings, private audiences they were, for once she learned I had conquered the tongue, she was eager to talk with me. I sweated, dreading questions about my former life which I could not answer. Happily for my peace, old Khin-nom warned her that my memories were yet few and fragmentary, that the many lives I had lived through on far, alien worlds lost in the vastness of the universe had dimmed and drowned out my memories of life in ancient Phaolon. Thank God for Khin-nom's tact! He had the delicate gift of adroit distortions of unpleasant truths that could have made his fortune in diplomacy.

I could never figure him out, the wily old sage. Was he on my side, or against me? I always wondered what he really thought about me; I can't believe he thought me truly Chong the Mighty come again, and many were the sly, suave insinuations he delivered in this direction; however, he never sought to expose me for an interstellar impostor, and at times, as above, in preface to my first private audience with Niamh, he subtly protected me from exposure.

Like most philosophers, he was himself an enigma.

My first audience was held under semiformal conditions, in an antechamber to the private apartments of the princess. It was neither a completely informal tête-à-tête, nor a completely formal state audience. Curious as any young girl, the princess merely wanted to talk to me and ask me questions.

She wore a simple robe of some light, clinging white stuff that reminded me of samite, and she sat on a raised cushion, feet curled under her like a child. I was sweating and uncomfortable in the stiff brocades tradition required of one on such an occasion; and, from time to time, irked by the weight of gem-studded cuff-bands and the constriction of a high, tight collar stiffened with gold wire, I twitched about, red-faced and suffering. From the bland expression on her flower-like face and the scarcely concealed flash of mischief in her great eyes, I suspect the girl took an impish relish in my obvious discomfiture.

I felt far more comfortable the next day, when, dressed in warrior's harness, I accompanied her on a riding expedition. The elf-knights of Phaolon wear begemmed and plumed garments, as I have already described; such fancy dress might make them look suitable for a road show production of *A Midsummer Night's Dream*, but the gaudy costumes are hardly fit for fighting in. Fortunately, Chong's era lay in simpler times, and it was the shrewd notion of the princess that I would feel more at home in the simple scale tunic, swash-topped boots, plate girdle, and cloak of my own epoch. Actually, I still felt rather like a fugitive from a masquerade ball, but the simpler harness of Chong's period was less confining, less ornate and ridiculous, and afforded me greater ease of movement.

"Riding" on the World of the Green Star is a less-than-accurate term. Since the Laonese dwell in tree-cities far above the ground, and shun the land surface due to the terrible predators that prowl the floor of the continent-sized forests, their steed of choice is winged rather than hooved. I was somewhat timorous of mounting these fantastical flying coursers, due as much to my inexperience in the saddle as to a natural reluctance to swooping giddily through the air astride nothing more substantial than an enormous butterfly. But there was no hope for it, and a royal invitation is the same as a royal command. And it ill-befitted the national hero of Phaolon to admit he was afraid of heights!

The princess rode in a floating bubble drawn by immense moths called *dhua*. These fantastic creatures had long tubular bodies the size of Terrene crocodiles, but banded with topaz dusted with powdered diamond, their heads great featureless casques of glistening black horn with huge compound eyes like faceted sapphires, and dainty antennae of scarlet, knobbed at the tip with puff-balls of velvet. They were weird and exquisite and looked horribly frail to support such weight as human bodies; but then, at a flick of the reins, they unfolded colossal satiny wings of gorgeous emerald and sunset crimson, wings as huge as yacht sails!

The chariot in which the princess rode was a thin fluted shell of glossy pearl drawn by a team of matched *dhua*. The knights of her entourage and myself were saddled upon the backs of the titanic moths. These saddles were like highchairs, with back supports and high pommels, fashioned of scarlet lizard-hide stretched tightly over weightless wicker frames. We were seated well forward of the immense gauzy wings, directly behind the glistening ovoid heads of our fantastical steeds, and, much to my relief, we were belted securely to the saddles by saftey straps so that it was all but impossible to fall out.

To limber up the lax, long-unused muscles of this new body of mine, I had long since formed the habit of working out with Panthon and the other warriors in my service every afternoon, following the conclusion of each language lesson. I had practiced with broadsword and buckler, bow and javelin, until my muscle tone was restored and my body glowed with health and vigor.

Employing these antique weapons with which, of course, I had never been familiar, I had noticed an odd phenomenon. That is, while I was not conscious of any familiarity in swordsmanship or archery, the thews and sinews of my body seemed somehow to "know" these weapons and without even thinking about it I blocked the blows of my friendly opponents and dealt them a few shrewd strokes of my own.

It was as if the use of the Laonese weapons had been so deeply ingrained in the habit patterns of the former resident of this flesh, that when I permitted my body to respond automatically to an exercise duel, my very muscles somehow "remembered" their facilities of old. I suppose this is not so remarkable as it seemed to me at the time; after all, the *brain* of Chong the Mighty still lived, although his conscious mind had been replaced by my own. Still, it was an uncanny sensation, feeling your limbs

T. KIRK

react to habit patterns your consciousness knew nothing of!

The same strange feeling of unconscious familiarity took possession of me from the moment I was strapped into the high saddle of my *dhua*. Chong had flown these fantastical creatures a thousand times, and his body knew to a nicety each delicate flick or tension of the reins, and how to guide the graceful courser of the air in flight. After a brief initial awkwardness, I relaxed, and let my body guide the *dhua* on its winged way.

We floated through a gold and emerald twilight world of leafy shadows and shafts of shining sunlight. About us in every direction stretched hazy distances of bough and blossom. The air had a crisp, cool tang; the weightlessness of flight was exhilarating; we soared and swooped and floated with the effortless ease of a child's dream of magic flight. I felt like an elf-knight accompanying Titania on a fairy quest. . . .

The occasion was an annual event in the court calendar. Once each year the gorgeous gigantic dragonflies the Laonese call *zaiph* vie to mate with their winged queen. The mating ritual is called "The Dance of the *Zaiph*," and it was in truth weird and wondrous, beautiful and strange beyond the reach of words.

The queen was an immense golden thing of shimmering loveliness, twice again the size of the glittering males that strove to win her favors. Elfin huntsmen in velvet green with feathered caps had caged her, awaiting our arrival to release the royal beauty. All about, on the immense branches, male *zaiph* hovered, trilling their unearthly serenade.

As Niamh floated near in her airy chariot, and gave the signal with a gesture of her dainty silver riding whip, the cage flew open and the gorgeous queen spread wings of sheeted opal and launched her golden flash toward the heavens. In the next instant, half a hundred dragon swains shot from their perches, whirling aloft in a glitter of metallic splendor. We of the court sounded crystal hunting horns and soared to match the ascent of the spiral horde that whirled skyward in a trail behind the golden queen.

The splendid chase was an experience no Terrene hunt could match for exquisite thrill or intoxicating beauty. We rode up vast sunshafts of incandescent jade, through clouds of golden leaves, on the traces of soaring dragonflies as huge as stallions. The wind sang about us, whipping our

cloaks like wings. The enormous vans of our moth-steeds
floated like sails of fantastic tapestry. Leaves like sheeted
foil swept past us: then we were above the branches in a
misty void of opal vapor that fell away to the world's
edge.

Far, far aloft, pinned to the dim emerald star like a
winged brooch of flashing gold, the queen hung, outpacing
all her suitors save one splendid tawny-crimson brute
whose head was a horned helm of blazing amethyst. As
we soared below their skyey height they circled each
other—then clung, mating in sunshot ecstasy, like brilliant gods. In the moment of their orgasm, their opal vans
froze motionless. Locked in dual embrace they fell from
that jade eminence, blazing like meteors down the vapory
sky; fell flaming from our sight, dwindling below amidst
the leafage of the world-tall trees.

I floated beside Niamh's chariot. Her face was flushed
with the thrill of the chase, eyes aflame with rapture. And
in that moment our eyes looked deep into each other's,
and her virginal soul was naked to my gaze.

An instant only; then silken lashes veiled the maiden
candor of her joy and her heart-shaped face flushed crimson.

But in that instant, I loved her, and she knew it.

Chapter 8

SWORD AGAINST DRAGON

The chase done, we dismounted on the branch of a nearby tree for a sort of court picnic.

The giant trees of the World of the Green Star are unbelievable in height and girth. In comparison, men and women shrink to mote-size, like ants next to skyscrapers. The main branches of these forest colossuses are broader than twelve-lane highways and sturdy enough to support entire cities. The branches whereat we paused for our midday meal, however, were less huge—say, of the width of ordinary streets.

Our perch was not really precarious. The branches are gnarled and whorled and knotted, their sheaths of bark rough and coarse as broken rock face. One would have to be amazingly clumsy to slip or fall—and the Laonese are nimble as mountain goats, utterly unafraid of heights, with a superb sense of balance.

All about us hung leaves the size of tents, lucently golden like vast sheets of antique parchment; emerald shafts of sun, striking down through filtering layers of leafage, drowned us in a dreamy haze of green-gold twilight.

While grooms tethered our *dhua* to twigs, domestics unpacked delectable food and drink from saddlebags. The lunch was a picnic sort of thing, of zesty, spicy oddments—narrow crusty cakes savory of almond paste, tiny cubes like anchovy sandwiches, slices and crisps of pickled fruit—all washed down with a foamy, effervescent drink that had the dry sparkle of champagne and the robust heartiness of dark beer.

We ate, clustered apart in couples and trios, scattered here and there about the branch. I had been favored with the honor of riding with the princess during the Dance of the *Zaiph*, now another was favored as her luncheon companion: a languid, lisping youth of ancient lineage and high rank named Awaiiomna, whom I particularly detested. The slender, elfin Laonese males are generally graceful and effeminate, but this particular princeling was foppish, limp-wristed and catty to a fault.

He and the princess retired to an upper curve of the bough, accompanied by Niamh's maid; half-hidden from us by a screen of lucent gold leaves, I could not watch them with a jealous eye, as I longed to—I could only sit, seething, straining my ears to catch Awaiiomna's sly whispers, and boiling with rude fury at Niamh's frequent bursts of tinkling laughter.

My own luncheon companion was the High Bonze Eloigam, a dour priest whose conversation consisted of enigmatic homilies spiced with obscure texts from the Laonese scriptures. I understood hardly a word he said, and the grunts and nods and growls I gave in answer to his attempts at conversation must have been equally uninformative.

The High Bonze, it seemed, had been literally aching to get my ear, for he had a thousand and one queries of philosophic or metaphysical nature to try on me. In retrospect, I can sympathize with the crusty old cleric, for, after all, as one who had certainly passed through the portals of life and death and rebirth, I must have been a tempting potential source of enlightenment on the nature of the gods, the astral terrain of the World Above, and all the more arcane secrets of super-nature.

"The World Above," incidentally, is the name the Laonese give their conception of heaven. I suppose it is only natural for the theological speculations of a cloud-wrapped planet to situate the country of the gods beyond the eternal cloudbanks; thus, at any rate, was the Laonese theory. I have never bothered to look very deeply into the native religion, a subject of great complexity at best, with endless pantheons of divinities, their various aspects and avatars, their multiplex natures each enshrined in a separate configuration, wrapped in its own apocalypse. Between the ultimate godhead and ordinary man, as well, are rank upon rank of saints and sages, prophets and miracle workers, angels and *apsaras* (a sort of Laonese version of valkyries), symbolic monsters, tutelary spirits, ancestral and clannish totem beasts, nature elementals, and guardian genies. The subject is worth a lifetime of study, for one so inclined.

At any rate, in my surly mood, I was struggling to make what answer I could to the probing questions of the High Bonze, coping as best I could with a spotty vocabulary unsuited to dealing with the higher matters of theologies, when a startling shriek of terror interrupted the meal and shattered the leafy tranquility of the idyllic scene.

It was Niamh's voice!

Once again, the trained reflexes of my warrior's body functioned automatically, bringing me to my feet in a lithe surge of rippling thews. Snatching my sword from its shoulder baldric, I nimbly sprang up the ascending coil of the branch, past lunching couples and trios frozen in sudden shock.

I shouldered through the screen of golden leaves to see a tableau of ultimate horror.

Niamh stood against a twig-stem the width of a sapling, luminous amber eyes dark and enormous against the pallor of her drawn visage. At her feet, cowering like a terror-stricken child, crouched the trembling highborn youth who had been her companion. He was gibbering in fright, mouth wet and working, hands futilely pawing at empty air as if to push from sight the monster that menaced them.

It was a *ythid,* the most fearsome carnivore of the World of the Green Star. Imagine a scarlet reptile twice the length of a full-grown tiger, with a saw-tooth spine and lashing barbed tail, and you will have a picture of the thing.

With three pairs of sucker-disked claws, it clung to the up-curve of the dwindling bough. It glared down at the two helpless victims, mindless ferocity in its burning green eyes. The hooked snout snuffed the air, scarlet jaws parting to reveal a double row of fangs like curved daggers.

As I watched, the tree dragon glided toward its quarry, crouching on its six legs for the pounce.

No one else was near enough to help; my sword glittered naked in my hand: it was up to me!

Silence stretched taut to the breaking point. Steely

sinews writhed and bunched in the sextuple shoulders, as the monstrous *ythid* gathered itself to leap upon the two.

The sword in my hand was a toy, a mere rapier with a slim blade of that strange, supple glass-clear metal the Laonese use instead of ferrous ore. Now I had cause to bitterly regret laying aside my mighty broadsword before departure, thinking it too heavy and cumbersome for the chase.

But—glittering toy or not—the sword was all I had. And it would have to do.

I hurled myself in the path of the *ythid*, splitting the silence with a deafening bellow!

My glass blade flashed and twinkled, slicing the air as I flicked the razory length across the hooked snout of the crouching reptile. Yellow gore spurted: the *ythid* recoiled with a squeal of surprise and anguish loud as a steam whistle.

I sprang to one side as it extended its long neck, snapping viciously at empty air where I had been a split second before. Whirling like a dancer, I slashed at the scarlet-mailed shoulder nearest me; again yellow blood squirted from the cut.

It gave voice to an ear-splitting screech and clawed at me, striking with blurring speed. I leaped back as hooked claws ripped open my leather tunic from throat to groin, merely grazing my flesh. Perspiration popped out on my brow; one good stroke of those keen sharp claws would disembowel me in an instant.

Fighting by pure instinct, I cut down at the extended paw, and caught it a shrewd blow at the wrist joint. Again, gore splashed from the wound—glistening, oily dragon blood, curiously yellow, like molten topaz.

Suddenly the thing reared up, using its terminal limbs to hold it secure to the curve of the bough. I swung at a scarlet forepaw—missed—drew back for another try— and felt an iron grip crush my midsection!

One of the middle limbs had caught me in its grasp, hooked claws tightening like a vise.

The squalling brute jerked me off my feet and up into the air. The crushing pressure of those closing claws was driving the air from me; my face blackened; I gasped for breath.

The grinning saurian jaws swung down toward me, hideous fangs glistening wetly, eyes mad with pain and blood-lust. The foul breath of the thing blew like a hot, moist, fetid wind directly in my face. The stench of the dragon's breath was sickening.

My lungs ached for air; my gaze dimmed in a swimming blur; as my strength ebbed, I cut again and again at the wrist that held me, hacking through sinew and tendon and tough scaly hide. Yellow gore splattered me. Death was near. I fought on.

The eyes of the *ythid* stared directly into mine, vast empty orbs of soulless green flame, burning with cold lust. In another second those drooling jaws would close about me with a sickening crunch, snuffing out my life. Would I die, then, go drifting down into darkness? Or would my far-wandering spirit drift Earthward down the starways, leaving the World of the Green Star behind, lost in the star-gemmed infinity of space?

Then one glaring green lamp of an eye was extinguished!

From nowhere a black feathered arrow appeared, thrumming in the center of the ruined orb, which dissolved, leaking slow, gelatinous tears of tawny gore.

The *ythid* screamed, rearing at the intolerable pain!

The barbed arrow must have pierced the eye itself, probing like a flaming brand into the very brain.

The scarlet tree dragon convulsed, lashing out in its agony until the whole branch quivered.

As it convulsed in agony, the *ythid* opened its claws, which were slowly crushing the life out of me. The claws sprung wide—the beast dropped me. I bounced, rolled, clutched the rough bark, and clung to the branch. It whipped wildly, as the scarlet dragon threshed in the madness of its death agony.

My sight dimmed, lungs panting, gasping, as I drank deep of fresh, tangy air. Staring around, I saw my faithful Panthon at the base of the branch, lifting his bow to loose a second black feathered shaft at the flopping, squalling *ythid*.

It sank to the feather in the brute's gullet as the jaws strained open for another screech. The second barbed arrow must have transfixed the dragon brain, for it convulsed as if touched by the lash of lightning.

Alas, Panthon! In your fervor to save me from the jaws of the *ythid*, you wrought another, no less fearful, doom!

For, as the dying brute convulsed in its death spasm,

the spike-tipped tail lashed out, curling about the twig to which my beloved princess clung in a paralysis of fear.

It snapped, and she fell from the thrumming branch with one sharp, despairing cry that pierced my heart.

Exhausted, gasping breath into my starved limbs, my sword fallen from my hands, smeared from top to toe with yellow dragon gore, I was a sorry portrait of a dragon battling hero at that moment.

But I did not pause to think. I saw her fall, vanishing from sight in a twinkling, and the pang went through me, numbing my brain with calamity. One quick glimpse of her white face and wide, frightened eyes—one quick cry of despair—and the woman I loved was gone from me.

Staggering to my feet, I cried out her name. And then I hurled myself from the branch, and fell like a stone into the dim, world-deep abyss of leafy gloom—

Chapter 9

CAUGHT IN THE WEB

Probably everyone has experienced the nightmare of falling endlessly. Usually the dream breaks just before the moment of impact—just before flesh pulps, brain matter squirts from shattered skull, and limbs break sickeningly.

That dream of horror I lived now. Falling ... falling ... down and down ... vast branches whirling past me ... canopy of gold-tissue leaves whipping by ... shadowy gulf of doom yawning beneath me as I hurtled into the giddy abyss.

What lent an exquisite frisson to the nightmare was that I could actually see my princess beneath me, like a falling flower, bright chase-tunic fluttering tulip-yellow, carnation-red.

She was far beneath, me, turning head over heels in a tumble of bare ivory limbs and a blur of spun-silver hair.

I knew we would not live to suffer the hideous death of hurtling down to shatter against the monster roots at the bottom of the gulf. Already I was panting for breath, the rapidly accelerating speed of my fall whipping the air past mouth and nostrils too swift for me to breathe. I had read of those who fall from great heights, and I knew their death was swift and merciful—from suffocation. They did not live to feel the impact as flesh mangled against sharp stones below. And the branch from which she had been flung—the branch from which I had sprung after her—must have been three miles or more aloft.

We would be dead, both of us, long before we struck the ground.

My eyes watered in the hissing wind of my fall; vision blurred; I blinked.

And in the next instant, crashed into some unglimpsed obstacle with stunning force. And knew no more.

When I awoke I was bruised and numb and aching in every thew. Some strange constriction held me, and some strange pressure filled my head; my face felt hot and congested and I had a problem breathing. My heart labored within my breast.

I opened my eyes and stared straight downward into an abyss of gloom!

A moment of vertigo and madness seized me. Few experiences can be more nightmarish than awakening from a swoon to find yourself hanging upside down above a terrific gulf.

I steadied my nerves with an effort of will, forcing myself to unclench my squeezed tight eyes. I looked down again: the floor of the forest was a mile beneath me, lost in impenetrable darkness. Few and faint are the shafts of emerald sun that sink through the infinity of leaves to lighten the everlasting gloom of the surface of the weird world of Himalaya-tall trees.

But I did not see the pitiful, broken body of my love below me; so there was still hope.

In what was I entangled? It felt rather like a net. But something bound me tight—some constriction had caught and broken my fall. It was a wonder the impact of that collision had not been my death: nonetheless, I yet lived.

I craned and kicked and struggled about, and saw to my utter amazement that I was entangled in the torn, sticky meshes of a spiderweb!

True, the web must have measured five miles across—for such was the distance between the tree from which I had hurtled and its nearest neighbor—but it was a web, just the same.

My imagination quailed, flinching from a guess as to the size of the spider which had spun so unthinkable a web. Think of it yourself—a web longer than the Golden Gate Bridge!

The cables of the mesh nearest me were inches thick, spun of a gluey stuff yellowy-white in color. I could make out no texture or braiding to the strands: they were for all the world like nothing more than ropes of rubber cement—but half-a-hand thick, and miles in length!

The impact of my fall had torn the webwork mesh and the flexive, gluey cabling had stretched to the thrust—and it was this springy "give" that had broken my fall without breaking my bones.

The relief of knowing I was safe made me giddy—I laughed in hysteria. *Safe*—if you can call yourself safe, stuck in a Brobdingnagian spiderweb a mile in the sky!

Then, looking about, my heart leaped in a throat-stopping throb of joy. For there, a dozen yards away, dangling pale and limp, still unconscious, was—*Niamh!*

She did not seem to be injured. She hung in her swoon, bright silver hair a silken banner rippling faintly in the breeze, her scarlet raiment torn and disarranged, revealing mellow glimpses of smooth thigh and sleek, soft shoulder. But, although unconscious, her shallow breasts rose and fell as she breathed and her silken eyelids fluttered as if stirring towards wakefulness.

Then it was that I sensed an ominous vibration moving down the taut cables of the web.

The spiders which haunt the worldwide forests of the Laonese planet are known as the *xoph*. I did not know this at the time, but learned the word later.

The pressure of our fall into its miles-wide web had aroused the monster from its mindless slumber.

Now, immense white furred legs feeling delicately along the strand, it blindly sought to ascertain our position. I held my breath in suspense, knowing that the slightest involuntary motion would communicate itself throughout the webwork.

Only the gods of the World Above knew how close—or how far away—the monster spider made its hideous lair. If it were akin to the arachnida of my own far-off world, it could be at the very center of the web, curled in a silken pocket, or at the extremity of the strands.

How near were *we* to the center?

It was impossible to say: in the green-gold gloom I could hardly see the soaring, dark vastness that was the next tree—but we were quite some distance from our own. The huge crawling thing might be half a mile distant —or several miles. It might take it but minutes to scuttle down the wobbling strand to where we dangled like fruit ripe for the picking—or hours!

I began to strive against my sticky bonds. If we could get loose now—if we could clamber down the strand to reach our tree in time—perhaps we could escape the attack of the loathsome *xoph*.

If not, then truly we were doomed. For I had lost my sword, and would have to fight the thing with my bare hands.

If we could not reach the nearest tree before the hideous thing was upon us, then our luck in landing amidst the great web was but a cruel jest of fate, who had thus spared us a quick, merciful death from suffocation to die slowly and horribly in the clutches of the gigantic *xoph*, which would drink our blood drop by drop, in slow, agonizing sips, through its horrible hollow fangs.

Niamh awoke from her swoon during my struggle to free myself from the gluey grip of the web.

One wide-eyed glance about her in terror, and the gallant-hearted girl summoned her courage and lay quietly watching me. Like all denizens of this world, she knew the dreaded *xoph* and the slow and ghastly death they bring their helpless victims. She knew that as I fought and tore against the constriction of my bonds I was signaling our position to the monstrous bloated thing that crouched listening somewhere not far off in the leafy whispering gloom.

Child of her strange and beautiful and savage world, she knew that we must fight against death, or wait supinely for the bitter kiss of the horrible hollow fangs.

For an interminable time, I struggled against the gluey substance that bound me. And all the while there came down the long cable-like strands of the web that distant tremor that announced the coming of the monster arachnid in whose net we lay entangled. With every moment that passed, the albino vampire came nearer—nearer!

I fought on: there was nothing else to do. If fate so willed, I would die still fighting to save the woman I loved from the slavering jaws that thirsted to drink her blood. It might well be that my fight would prove hopeless in the end; but I would face the judgment of whatever gods might be, without shame, my honor unstained, knowing that however I had failed, at least I had done my best.

No man can do more than his best.

At length I managed to extricate myself from the cling-ing web. And for this I owe thanks to the scarlet *ythid* loyal Panthon had slain with his arrow. For in my strug-gles with the tree dragon, my glass rapier had pierced its mailed hide again and again, drenching me from head to toe in reeking dragon blood.

The yellow gore stunk abominably, and I was so be-smeared with the stuff that I resembled a refugee from battlefield or charnel house. But the oily liquid which stained my limbs resisted the adhesive properties of the sticky web and gave me more freedom of movement than I might otherwise have enjoyed.

Crawling free from the strands, I climbed along the web to where Niamh lay hopelessly entangled.

"Do not be afraid," I said. "We still have a chance."

The brave girl stared up at me. Her face was pale but self-composed, and her amber eyes shone with unquenched courage.

"I am not afraid," she said, "for you are with me."

I could think of no reply to this astounding testimony of faith, but inwardly I prayed to the grim gods that Niamh's faith in me was not misplaced!

In its death convulsions, the *ythid* had not besplattered the princess with its gore. But the portions of the giant web which entangled her adhered more to her garments than to her flesh; thus, setting her free was a compara-tively simple matter of tearing away most of what remained of her robes. It left her clad in garments whose brevity would not have pleased modesty or convention: but at least she was free.

"What can we do now?" she asked.

It was a dilemma. I did not care to linger here, awaiting the approach of the monstrous spider, for it would result in a hopeless struggle. I was unarmed, with nothing to pit against the ferocity of the *xoph* but sheer strength alone. And the iron vigor of my thews would prove a puny de-fense against the fanged jaws of the monster denizen of this colossal web.

Our only recourse seemed to be to flee along the web, hoping to reach the nearest tree before the brute was upon us. Luckily, this was a task far less difficult than it may sound to you. For while we were thousands of feet above the forest floor, the Laonese are racially immune to the vertigo that would have left all but the boldest adventurer of my distant planet helpless in a paralysis of giddy terror. And when I had inherited the body of Chong, I had inherited as well his cool nerve and the fearlessness for heights that was an attribute of his race.

As well, the cable strand along which we must travel was far thicker than you might think. While the web strands themselves were of thicknesses that varied from the width of a man's finger to the width of his thigh, the great anchor cables that secured the web to the tree trunks were truly colossal, as big around as tree trunks on my own world, and so sticky there was very little problem of falling.

So we began to inch our way along the cable, going as swiftly as was humanly possible, but not so swiftly as we could have wished. For a strange chittering sounded from behind us, a dry, hollow sound, like the pattering of crisp leaves. And we looked over our shoulders into a face of frightful horror.

The huge spider had advanced stealthily upon us while I had been busied freeing Niamh—and in the next instant it was upon us in a rush, glittering eyes blazing soullessly into mine, horny mandibles clashing at my throat!

Chapter 10

IN THE GRIP OF THE XOPH

Even now my flesh creeps with horror as memory conjures up that moment of transcendent fright. I am sure I shall relive that nightmare battle on the mile-high web in my dreams for years to come.

Picture for yourself our predicament. We stood, insecurely perched on a spiderweb thousands of feet in the air. With every step—with every slightest motion—the taut cable strand swayed and trembled under our feet. Although the monstrous strand was as thick as a tree trunk, the slightest misstep could hurl us from our precarious perch to a horrible death amid the titanic roots far below us, lost in the impenetrable gloom of the forest floor.

And there, upon that giddy, swaying strand, we faced bare-handedly a monster so fearful and ferocious that I would willingly have challenged a pride of lions, armed only with a peashooter, if I but had a choice. Now did I truly have reason to regret the loss of my sword. It had been only a flimsy dress rapier, and not my mighty two-handed broadsword, but in such a predicament I would have felt myself fortunate to be armed even with a dagger.

As for the thing I faced and must fight, words alone cannot convey its frightfulness or ferocity. Imagine a spider grown to the proportions of an elephant and you will have only the faintest conception of the multi-legged horror that loomed before us.

The *xoph* was unspeakably repulsive and loathsome to the sight. Its cylindrical body was encased in a horny carapace of slimy, glistening chitin as tough as armorplate. This oily thorax terminated in the obscene bulge of its abdomen, which hung down beneath it, the egg sac hideously bloated and swollen. Like Terrene spiders, the *xoph* has eight jointed legs clad in greasy chitin, terminating in multiple claws; and it hung aloft on these towering skeletal limbs, glaring down upon us with eyes like clusters of black jewels—eyes aflame with cold ferocity and mindless lust.

The stench of the spider-thing was overpowering, a sickening reek of decay and corruption like an open sewer. But what made the *xoph* so loathsome was that it was snowy-white, a repulsive albino thing, its stalk-like legs and bloated belly shaggy with stinking white fur, besoiled with oily droppings.

Its face was a monstrous mask of indescribable horror. It bore not the slightest resemblance to the face of beast or man, bird or reptile. It was a shield-shaped casque of greasy chitin, lobed and crescentiform, rising to either side of the central mouth orifice in twin bosses or stubby horns. The eyes of the thing were completely inhuman, swollen structures of many-faced ebon crystal, glittering with blood-lust. And, instead of a mouth, the monster had a drooling slit which worked to and fro obscenely. From the corners of this repulsive orifice two jointed mandibles thrust clackingly at me—they were as large as the arms of a full-grown man, ending in curious multiplex claws which rubbed and rasped and clicked together in continuous motion.

It was in the grip of the dexter mandible that I was held, writhing helplessly. The chitinous claw resembled the pincers of a gigantic albino crab, with saw-toothed edges of durable horny stuff. The grip of the mandible was crushing and I feel certain that the pincers would have torn off my arm had it not been for the fortunate fact that the mandible had gripped me on the upper arm, just where I wore an armlet of heavy silver.

Niahm screamed in hopeless despair as the stinking thing pounced upon us with a rush, seizing me in its foremandible. I, too, felt a moment of sickening despair as the *xoph* tore me from the sticky web strand with a surge of irresistible strength. I hung there above the web, completely helpless in the crushing grip of the spider monster, dangling like a mouse from the jaws of a cat.

Had it been able to grasp me as well with its other fore-mandible, there is no slightest doubt in my mind but

that the giant spider could have torn me in half with a
a single flexing of its foreclaws. But as it was, the mandibles
branched from either side of that awful, drooling, lipless slit
of a mouth, and the width of this orifice was such that the
second mandible could not easily get a grip on me, although
it scissored with a horrible rasping click only inches from
my legs, which swung to and fro as the albino spider-thing
swung me about.

Ere long, giving up any further attempt to seize me
with both mandibles, it brought the dexter mandible near
that gruesomely slavering mouth slit. Within the fleshless
maw I could see multiple-horned tusk-rows grinding. If
once the monster spider had me in its bony jaws, my flesh
would be mangled to pulp in an instant.

As it was, the nameless slime excreted from the working jaws dripped upon my thighs. I have no notion of
what vicious acid or digestive chemical the *xoph* secretes,
but the slobber which fell on my flesh stung like fury and
the foul, stinking breath that blew from the triple-fanged
inner maw was unspeakably vile.

I realized instantly what the monster spider was attempting to do. Luckily, it was only my left arm that was
helplessly caught in the grip of the mandible, and right
arm and both legs were free. Swinging my body up, I
planted both booted feet against the horny helm of the
spider's face, one above and one below the hideous, slavering mouth orifice. Bracing myself, I resisted with all my
strength the *xoph*'s attempt to cram me into its clashing
jaws, now only inches from my flesh.

In all the annals of fantasy and romance, was ever a
hero caught in such a hopeless predicament? I clung there,
pushing with all the strength of my legs against the face of
the monster, as it strove again and again to thrust me into
the reach of those tusked and clashing jaws.

The steely strength of my thigh muscles was great—but
how long could I stave off the irresistible ferocity of the
giant spider? Surely, fight as best I could, I would in time
reach the dregs of my strength, and as my vigor was
exhausted, I would be forced into the clashing jaws to be
mangled to ribbons.

There was no hope of rescue. I was unarmed—Niamh,
as well, bore no weapon, and the frail strength of her
slender body could do naught to assist me. Yet I fought

on with grim, dogged determination, although I knew all too well that it was only a matter of time. Already the muscles of thigh and calf ached from the strain: if only I had some weapon, any weapon at all! For my right hand was free. . . .

My right hand was free!

Without a moment's hesitation, I balled my right hand into a fist and drove it smashing down like a hammer into the bulging complex eye nearest me!

The glittering faceted eye of the spider-thing was of some hard crystalline stuff, but like crystal it was also fragile. Sheer warrior instinct had led me to the discovery of the one fatal weakness of the chitin-armored *xoph*—the eyes!

In a trice I had hammered the monster's left eye to crumpled ruin. The multiplex inner structure broke beneath my smashing blows like hard panes of wax in an immense honeycomb. A colorless, oily fluid leaked from the ruined eye of the giant spider.

I know not whether the albino monster was capable of feeling pain, but it uttered a high, thin, piercing shriek. It shook its two-horned head like a maddened thing, all but dislodging me from where I clung. The mandible that held me helpless bore down with shearing force on my left arm, and I would have been crippled in an instant, had it not been for the arm-ring of heavy metal I wore clasped high about my biceps. As it was, the smooth silver of the ring grated and squealed under the pressure as the saw-toothed mandible crunched down in maddened fury on my arm.

Now I swung myself about, with some difficulty, striving to reach the many-faceted eye that bulged out like a swollen mass of black crystals on the other side of the monstrous horny head. But from the position in which I was held, the other eye was beyond my reach.

Risking all on a desperate gamble, I swung about. Bracing myself with but one foot against the mandible that strove to force me into the drooling maw, I drove the other booted foot crashing into the monster's second eye!

It squealed in an ear-splitting shriek of fury as my heel crunched through the complex structure. The globular eye broke in a smear of oily ruin—

And the *xoph*, stung at last with stabbing pain, threshed to and fro in blind agony—

And dropped me!

I struck the thick anchor cable to which the spider clung and would have bounced from it, hurtling into the dim gloom-drowned abyss below, had it not been that the leather of my war harness clung to the adhesive cable.

Niamh was at my side in an instant, even as the adhesion of the cable was yielding to my weight. She caught my arm and half-lifted, half-dragged me to the topmost surface of the cable.

Thrusting her ahead of me, I staggered further out on the thick web strand. Behind us, the giant albino spider convulsed in maddened fury, furred legs thrusting, claws snapping at empty air, making the taut-stretched cable bounce and quiver to the frenzy of its convulsions.

We clambered away from the blinded thing with all possible speed, heading toward the nearer of the colossal trees, that soared above us like arboreal Everests.

"Will it follow us?" Niamh panted as she stumbled along the rise of the thrumming cable.

"Only the gods know that," I said. "But let us put what distance between us that we can—while we can!"

We both knew the brute could sense our whereabouts by its sensitivity to the vibrations of our movement as we scrambled up the web strand. Our only hope lay in the pain I had perhaps inflicted on the white furred monster. In its agony, it might not think to pursue us for some time—perhaps long enough for us to reach a more secure shelter among the boughs of the forest giant that rose before us like a tremendous wall of bark.

It took the two of us the better part of an hour to reach the crotch of one colossal branch, and whatever the reason, the monster *xoph* did not follow us up the great strand to where it was anchored to the tree.

The cable rose ever more steeply, like one of the support cables of a huge suspension bridge on my native world. Toward the last we were climbing with great difficulty up an almost vertical incline, and had it not been for the sticky goo wherewith the cable was surfaced, the feat would have been much more dangerous and difficult than it actually was.

But, after an interminable climb, we reached at last the safety of the crotch of a branch as broad as Times Square, and flung ourselves down, weary and trembling with exhaustion, faint from our exertions, but safe enough for a time.

But we were hopelessly lost—alone, unarmed, and helpless—in a strange world of shadowy terrors and numberless monsters against whose attack we had not the slightest means of defense.

And night was falling across the World of the Green Star.

Part III

THE BOOK OF SIONA
THE HUNTRESS

Chapter 11

A NIGHT IN A TREE

My life on Earth had been such that I had never been called upon to develop resourcefulness. A man of great wealth, surrounded by loyal servants, confined to my bed or a wheelchair, I had never been flung into circumstances where my very survival rested on my abilities to exist unaided in the wilderness.

But now I had nothing else to count on. At my side, worn and pale from the horrible experiences through which she had suffered, lay a beautiful young girl thrust by hapless fate under my protection.

Our predicament was an utterly hopeless one. Hungry, bone-weary from our battle against the albino *xoph*, trembling with fatigue from our exhausting climb up the monster spiderweb, marooned in a giant tree a mile above the world, we somehow had to find food and warmth and shelter from the night, and protection against the hideous predators who soon would be aprowl. And we had nothing but our bare hands!

Or did we? I still wore the leathern harness of a Laonese warrior, and the princess retained some tattered rags of her once-gorgeous gown, and perhaps something could be fashioned from the scraps. Necessity, they say, is the mother of invention; and few heroes of romance have suffered from the extremity of a need as great as ours.

The harness in which I was clad was a skimpy thing at best. An affair of belts and straps crisscrossed my naked chest; about my hips I wore a thick, heavy belt or girdle; my feet were shod in high, swash-top boots. Save for these, I was devoid of ornament or accouterment.

As for Niamh, she was left with mere tatters wherewith to clothe her modesty, and the brevity of her raiment was such as to leave naked her long, exquisitely slender legs and arms of mellow ivory; and, in truth, what little clothing she retained was full of rents through which gleamed glimpses of creamy flesh. A jeweled brooch, however, yet clung by its pin to the breast of her garment, and a large diamond, or some similar gemstone of smoky, lucent fire, adorned her hand.

As for my own harness, the heavy girdle clasped about my waist was fastened by a heavy buckle larger than a man's open hand. The tang of this buckle was a slender blade of coppery metal slightly more than four inches long. It might well serve as a decent dagger blade, if I had the means to sharpen it or to hone its edges.

Had we not been aloft in the branch of the sky-tall tree, I have no doubt but what I could have found a bit of flinty rock with a little searching, and could have honed my makeshift blade to a keen edge with some labor. One does not, however, look for stones in the upper branches of a tree.

I could not ignore this problem with any serenity of mind, for without a weapon of some sort we would be helpless to avoid the attack of the numberless predators with which the World of the Green Star swarmed. Our success in battling free of the monster spider was pure luck and largely accidental; I could not rely on fortune or Providence alone to extricate us safely from a second such encounter.

While Niamh rested, I rose to my feet and began prowling about the branch, looking for I know not what, but unable to rest easy without exploring our vicinity to discover what chance coupled with ingenuity might do to improve our situation. Food and drink were a problem, but the necessity of finding or making some manner of weapon occupied my thoughts to the exclusion of all else. Without a means of defending myself from attack, we would pass every moment in peril until help arrived from the Jewel City courtiers stranded somewhere aloft.

I explored first the crotch of the tree, the junction from which our branch sprang from the central trunk. The branch itself extruded from the trunk at a slight angle, and the place where it merged with the trunk formed a bowl-shaped hollow like a shallow pit. This slight depression contained a litter of dried leaves—each the size of outspread bedsheets. Here and there, pools of fresh rainwater had been caught in crevices in the rough bark. Thirst, therefore, would not be a problem of major concern, although lack of food might be.

After searching the crotch of the tree, I went further out on the branch to see what I might find. The branch extended for about a quarter of a mile, and, although it dwindled in width and angled upward at an ever-increasing incline, I found no especial difficulty in traversing its length, as the roughness of the bark made my progress easy enough—rather like walking across a field corrugated by the plow marks of a tractor.

Suddenly I stopped short. I had discovered we were not alone on our airy perch, and I tensed in grim anticipation of another unequal combat with a forest monster. The hulking shape before me was shrouded in the gloom of leaf-shadow: all I could make out was a gradual creeping movement and the rondure of a curved back, or so I at first assumed it to be. At length, however, and to my immense relief, I discovered the creature to be some sort of tree snail and probably of a harmless nature and a sluggish disposition. The snail, however, was the size of a full-grown dog, and its shell was a swelling hemisphere of pearly yellowish stuff, half as big as a bathtub.

The smallness of the inoffensive creature puzzled me a bit. If moths and dragonflies on this World of the Green Star grew to the size of horses and were large enough to ride upon, and if spiders attained a virtually elephantine bulk, you would think snails would grow on a comparable scale. This particular member of the species might, of course, be young; it might also belong to a dwarf genus.

Niamh, by now fully rested from her ordeal and either grown venturesome or reluctant to let me out of her sight, followed me to the terminus of the branch.

"It is only a *houoma*," she said. "It cannot harm us. In fact, they are good to eat."

I had not thought of the fact that not only is snail flesh edible and nutritive but, as the French know, delicious. Now that the princess mentioned the fact, I recalled that I had many times dined on *escargot* and found it a tempting delicacy. It was not difficult to slay the sluggish *houoma* and drag it back down to the crotch of the branch, and between us Niamh and I managed to break the shell away.

She pointed out that the shell, which had cloven neatly into two rounded halves, could serve as a bowl and that we could simmer the flesh of the snail in its own juices had we but the means of making a fire. Of course, like its near relatives the clam and the oyster, the meat of the snail is edible even when raw, but I would prefer to eat it cooked.

That presented another problem, but luckily not an insoluble one. It was not an easy task to make a fire with what we had to hand, but with patience I managed at length to strike sparks from the steel pin of Niamh's brooch and we found the soft inner lining of the tree bark as flammable as punk, while the dry tissue of the leaves flared up easily.

While Niamh cooked the succulent flesh of the *houoma* over a slow fire, filling the air with delicious odors, I busied myself with the remainder of the snail shell. The substance of the shell, while brittle, was remarkably tough. And while unshelling the *houoma*, I had found myself thinking about that hard horny shell, wondering if its cleanly broken edge would be durable enough so that I could hone and sharpen the tang of my belt buckle against it.

Copper is one of the softer metals, and by dint of patient and tedious effort I did indeed put an edge on my makeshift dagger blade. Or on half of it, anyway, leaving the blunter end to serve as my handgrip. This part of the dagger I bound with thin supple leather from my harness.

So, tired but safe enough for the present, we ate dinner.

The *houoma,* by the way, tasted remarkably like clam meat and made a satisfying and very filling meal, there was so much of it. We could have done with a bit of tomato sauce, though, or a twist of lemon, but I suppose Crusoes cannot be choosy.

After dinner we were ready for sleep. I built the fire up with enough bark fragments and scrapings to keep it burning steadily during the night. The bark did not flame up as wood would have done, but smoldered, turning to long-lasting coals. The warm orange-red glow of the coals would serve to keep night-prowling predators away, or so I hoped, and would shed enough heat to keep us comfortable should the night turn cool.

We curled up for the night on either side of our fire, using the less brittle of the huge yellow leaves to wrap around us like blankets. I was feeling a natural pride in my newfound skills of woodsmanship, although Niamh took my resourcefulness for granted and did not seem to think it worthy of praise. Of course, in her eyes I was Chong, a mighty hero out of the distant past, supremely able to cope with any manly feat. Only I knew that I was not the reincarnation of her hero but an impostor in a borrowed body. I did not dare disabuse her of her illusions. Before we fell asleep, we discussed our predicament, the hazards we would face in the days to come, and what few hopes we had. Niamh believed there was very little chance of our being rescued by those of her courtiers we had left behind on some branch far above us.

"They would not know where to look," she said quietly. "The world is large and full of terrors; and we are small and frail. They could not be expected to know we survived our fall, for none who fall from such a height ever survive."

"But surely they will search for us, nonetheless!" I argued. "I wonder they did not come flying down to find us hours ago—the descent to the web wherein we were entangled would only have taken them minutes, mounted on their *dhua.*"

She shook her head, silvery gloss of hair gleaming in the warm light of the coals.

"That they did not do so convinces me of what I had feared," she murmured, "and that is that they are marooned as helplessly as we. For the *dhua* are the natural prey of the fearsome *ythid,* and dread no beast with deeper terror. At the appearance of the tree dragon, the *dhua* would all have panicked, breaking tether and fleeing to the winds in their fright. I fear we can hope for no rescue from my people of Phaolon. . . ."

She sighed. The dim golden glow of the coals was warm on her lovely, heart-shaped face. Her silken lashes fluttered down, veiling the glory of her depthless amber eyes. And she slept. I stared long at the beautiful young girl with whom I had fallen so hopelessly in love and, when at length I drifted into sleep myself, my dreams were filled with visions of a slender maiden with limbs of mellow ivory and an elfin face enhaloed with a silken cloud of hair like floating, silvery gossamer.

My life on Earth had been secluded, protected, luxurious—and lovely. But I did not miss the safety and comforts of my Terrene existence. I would rather be where I was now, for all the discomforts and dangers, than return to Earth. I would rather dwell in a sky-high tree under the strange light of the Green Star, battling with naked hands against fearsome monsters, than go home to a dull, tedious life of boredom and ultimate futility.

For here I was a man, a splendid savage, not a hopeless cripple. Never before had I truly lived, tasting life with an appetite spiced with danger, feeling pride in my own prowess, knowing that each day I would face new and more horrendous perils, but knowing, at least, that I lived each moment to the hilt, with verve and gusto, with excitement and suspense, with romance and mystery and adventure, by the side of the most beautiful woman of two worlds!

Chapter 12

THE SCARLET ARROW

When I awoke, the sky above me was a stupendous and fantastic vista of colossal trees soaring to unthinkable heights, and the heavens themselves obscured by an infinite canopy of leaves that stretched from horizon to horizon. The light of the Green Star fell through rents in this enormous canopy in vagrant shafts of glowing jade, and the arboreal leafage itself was struck to an incandescence of burning gold.

The air was fresh and heady with a wine-like tang. My exertions of yesterday had left me aching with weariness and worn with fatigue. But a full belly and a night of deep slumber in the open air restored my vigor, and I rose with an exuberant vitality such as I have never known.

Niamh, too, rose refreshed and looking glorious. Gone was the jewelbox princess in her mandarin robes; in her place stood a lithe, long-legged girl with tousled hair, flushed cheeks, sparkling eyes, and joyous, merry laughter. A wild girl of the world-tall woods, true, in an abbreviated scrap of ragged raiment, but a fitting companion to the half-naked savage I had become, who faced the perils of the unknown forest armed only with a crude dagger!

We bathed in puddles of cold rainwater, breakfasted off the remnants of last night's dinner, and felt fit and ready to face whatever perils the new day might bring.

The more remote extremities of our branch extended in several directions in leafy twigs as huge as the foremast of a schooner. Some of these twigs brushed a much larger branch above us, and we resolved to attempt the ascent, having exhausted the resources our present milieu afforded

us. There was no way of telling what we might find on the
branch above us, and we could, of course, always return
to our present place, should we wish to.

I think it was the pure, childlike excitement of our
situation that urged us to explore as much of our strange
new world as we could. This life of hand-to-hand struggle
for survival against a savage world was as fresh and new
and intoxicating to Niamh as it was to me, for all that she
was native to the World of the Green Star. I once read of
an emperor of China whose life was so artificial and
circumscribed, so bound about by ritual and ceremony,
that it was said he never once in his long life saw a bush
or tree or field that was as nature had made it and not as
it had been trimmed and shaped and grown by generations
of gardeners. Niamh's life, she confided to me in her
artless way, had been no less artificial and sheltered. The
life of the court was all she had ever known; sleek courtiers, rigid conventions, ornamented surroundings, artificial
and sophisticated pleasures, were all that she had ever
known. Although we prowled a hostile wilderness teeming
with ferocious monsters, every moment pregnant with
unexpected terrors, she felt a sense of liberation and
freedom that was like a superb and golden wine to one
who had for too long subsisted on bland, insipid milk.

It was, I think, this sense of freedom which kept her
from worrying about the perils of our precarious position.
To be hopelessly lost in this world of giant trees, the prey
of unthinkable monsters, all chance of succor or rescue
slim, should have plunged so delicately reared a maiden
into an abyss of terror. But Niamh reacted to our predicament as if it were a spree, and the novelty of spending a
night in the wild, of slaying our own dinner, of exploring a
new world of mystery and beauty and savage peril she
found exhilarating. As we clambered out onto the extremities of our branch, her eyes were sparkling with mischief,
her cheeks flushed with excitement. With her ragged garments, long bare legs, smudged nose and tousled hair, she
was absurdly like an adventurous boy—very different
from the stiff, brocaded queen surrounded by a covey of
suave courtiers!

The upper branch, which we attained with some difficulty, was very much larger than the one whereon we had
spent the night. It was as wide as a four-lane highway and

it extended from the colossal trunk at a right angle, running parallel with the ground far below. It twisted and turned, curving and meandering away until lost from view in cloud-huge clumps of leaves.

We strolled out upon it for about a quarter of a mile. Again I felt a sense of awe at the enormity of the trees of this fantastic world—trees so immense they would have dwarfed into insignificance even the towering redwoods of my native Earth. And not for the first time did I wonder at the strange disproportion of men and trees on this World of the Green Star. I felt like a midge crawling on the branch of a mighty oak, and I pondered the mystery of the size of these arboreal colossuses. Could it be that these trees were actually of normal size, and that it was the dwellers upon the Green Star planet who were elf-small? It could be: when first I came hither, voyaging in my astral form, I had naturally assumed beings so manlike in their appearance must be manlike in their height. But the more I saw of the gigantic trees and the monstrously huge insects that dwelt upon them, the more I wondered. My astral form had been a mere spark of life—a point of consciousness, without reference of size. Had I perhaps lost all sense of proportion, mistakenly believing the Laonese to be of an height comparable to the inhabitants of my own world? Were they perhaps not a miniscule people, dwelling in trees which, to my physical self, would have seemed but average in their tallness?

To this question I had no answer then; nor can I answer it now. It was but one of the thousand mysteries I encountered on the World of the Green Star, not one of which I am able to explain.

We came suddenly upon a surprising marvel of beauty. It was an immense flower, waxen pale, its voluminous petals as creamy in hue as those of the camellia—but a thousand times larger than any flower that ever bloomed on my own world.

Niamh uttered a cry of delight and hovered entranced over the fantastic blossom. She confessed that her people seldom ventured far from the Jewel City, and that such flowers were unknown. She stroked the satiny petals, drinking in the heady perfume in an ecstasy of wonder.

The blossom sprouted from a tangle of rootlets like an air plant, and seemed to be parasitic. A thousand hairy green tendrils were insinuated between interstices of bark, anchoring the immense flower to the tree. The petals were half-open, like a trumpet lily or a morning glory, and from the deep center, where creamy white deepened to a ruddy hue, filaments of feathery scarlet floated limply. I stood, leaning on a branchlet, entranced at the mysterious beauty of the scene—the lovely, exquisite, elf-like girl hovering over the colossal flower: it was like an illustration from a fairy tale, and it would have demanded the genius of an Arthur Rackham or a Hannes Bok to capture the delicate nuances of the scene.

Suddenly Niamh shrieked in horror, and a scene of dreamlike loveliness turned upon the instant into a tableau of terror. For, the feathery scarlet filaments suddenly lashed out at the entranced girl like striking vipers. They coiled snakily about her wrists, holding both arms pinned in a grip of surprising tensile strength. I sprang forward, grasping her about her slim waist, and sought to pull her free of the cannibal blossom, but to no avail. The tentacles that slithered from the core of the monstrous blossom had a steely resilience that was astonishing.

As I fought and tore at the writhing tendrils, more and yet more coiled about the helpless girl. At the terminus of each scarlet length a clubbed anther hung. This organ was furred with minute spines and now that Niamh was tightly enmeshed in the coils, the anthers sought out her bare flesh. One pressed flatly against the rondure of her shoulder—another flattened against the small of her back—a third settled on her thigh.

She hung limply in the tenacious embrace of the giant flower as if in a swoon. As I grimly fought against the slithering tendrils, I felt a sudden dizziness cloud my brain. It was the heady perfume which hovered about us like a cloud of overpowering sweetness! My vision blurred; my heart thumped erratically. I fought on, senses dimming.

I had called the immense flower a parasite, not dreaming how close to the horrible fact my guess had gone. In truth, the colossal thing was a cannibal—a vampire—for now I saw, with a thrill of unbelieving horror and revulsion, that the furry anthers pressed like great sponges against the naked flesh of the dazed and swooning girl *gleamed wetly* of a sudden—and in the next instant I realized that the creamy pallor of the huge petals was flushing pinkly. *The vampire blossom was drinking her blood!*

I went mad with berserk rage, ripping at the hideous flower in a spasm of killing fury. Now I had cause to thank whatever shadowy and mysterious gods had guided me to this planet that I had honed that bit of copper into a crude dagger the night before. For the strength of my hands was as nothing against the rubbery constriction of the scarlet tendrils—but that sharp edge of copper cut like a saw blade into the flower flesh. In a few seconds I had managed to sever one of the anthers from its trunk, and I plucked the obscene thing from the small of Niamh's naked back, hurling it from me, turning my attention to the anther that pressed her shoulder, sucking her blood through a hundred hollow spines. All the while she hung limp and unprotesting in the net of scarlet tendrils: the narcotic fragrance of the vampire blossom had bemused her and she had drunk too deeply of the cloying, drug-like perfume.

I slashed through another filament and pulled the anther from her flesh. It pulled clear with a loathsome *sucking* sound, and where it had been pressed tightly against her skin it left a minute pattern of pinpricks, beaded with blood. I flung the wet thing from me, roaring.

But now tendrils lashed about my limbs as well, and I felt a sudden stinging sensation on my leg and, looking down, saw a great spongy anther pressed against my thigh just above the knee. It stung me like nettles, but the bitter kiss of the vampire blossom soon faded to a numbness. I ignored the thing fastened to my flesh, as I hacked away at the third of the anthers that yet clung to Niamh. But as I fought desperately, my head was swimming groggily and I knew the narcotic perfume of the horrible flower was overcoming me.

The monster blossom, I now knew, was no innocent and lovely flower but a grisly abnormality—a hideous plant-animal hybrid, whose blood-lusting nature was cunningly masked with nature's mimicry. Doubtless the loathsome thing was designed to resemble an ordinary flower, thus to lure the immense insect creatures of the World of the Green Star, the great *dhua*, the giant *zaiph*. Drawn by the sweet sorcery of its perfumed breath, the unsuspecting creatures would flutter near, either to be drugged into somnolence by the narcotic odor or to be caught by the hairy tendrils as they sought to rape away the sweetness hidden in the flower's honeyed heart.

But now the hybrid monstrosity had caught an unexpected treat in its silken trap. Human blood must have been a rare delight, for the now-crimson petals trembled with eager lust and the snaky tendrils lashed about the two of us in frenzied hunger. I sawed and slashed through the rubbery filaments with the dregs of my strength as the last flicker of consciousness waned. As my mind faded toward the twilight of drugged slumber, my last thought was that at least Niamh was unconscious, lulled by the narcotic fragrance, numbed by the anesthetic venom of the anthers, and endured no pain as the loathly vampire drained her blood. From that dim sleep she would never wake; her slumber would but deepen until she drifted over the dark portals of life and death, into a sleep from which there was no awakening. . . .

Then, as my hands faltered, as my grip loosened, as my eyelids drooped, something caught and held my waning attention.

A strange thing suddenly flicked into being, transfixing the stamen of the enormous blossom. I blinked at it, vaguely, without comprehension.

It was a scarlet arrow.

Chapter 13

OUTLAWS OF THE TREE

My vision obscured by a darkening haze, I blinked uncomprehendingly at the scarlet arrow which had so inexplicably appeared, transfixing the core of the vampire blossom as if conjured into being by an act of magic.

A blink of the eye, and another arrow—and another!—flicked into being, pinning the heart of the flower through and through!

And the flower—*screamed!* A high, unearthly squeal of rage and pain and terror, so shrill as to be almost inaudible. The blossom petals shivered—the root tendrils convulsed—the filaments that bound Niamh and myself tightened in a spasm, then relaxed. I tore free, and, although I staggered on unsteady legs, still half-drugged from the narcotic perfume I had inhaled, I lurched to where Niamh's limp body dangled in the flower's obscene embrace, and tore her from the relaxing grip of the tendrils.

Men melted into being all around us, merging into sunlight from the gold-green gloom. They were taller, leaner, hardier-looking than the softer men who dwelt in jeweled Phaolon. They wore trim tunics and tight leggings of dark earth colors, umber, forest green, fawn, and russet. They wore peak-brimmed caps from which long feathers trailed, short cloaks of mottled suede, calf-high boots of supple leather. They were tanned and fit and hard-faced, with strong bare arms and bold, alert eyes. They looked, in fact, like Robin Hood's merry men, stepped from a painting by Howard Pyle. This resemblance was enhanced by the longbows and quivers of

scarlet arrows they wore, although most of them were armed with glass cutlasses and light javelins as well.

Like magical apparitions they melted out of the gloom. Without a word they helped me carry the half-conscious Niamh to a place of safety while their comrades hacked the flower to death with their curious crystal swords. The vampire blossom shrilled, lashed, and bled from a thousand wounds, its petals shredded; it lapsed into oozing ruin.

The exertion of pulling Niamh free had drained the last dregs of strength from my body. I slumped, staggered, and all but fell. One of the tall foresters gently took the girl's limp body from me; another steadied me as I sank to my knees. A third uncorked a belt canteen—made, I dimly realized, from a hollowed nut of size sufficient to hold nearly a pint of fluid—and held it to my lips. I drank strong red wine, bitter and resinous, but bracing.

Still too dazed to speak, I blinked as another figure emerged from the leaf-gloom—a tall, long-legged girl, bronzed and fit, with brown-gold eyes and gossamer mane of silver, dressed in an abbreviated tunic, leggings, and feathered cap. A girl among these woodland outlaws—and a girl of astonishing beauty?

I must have gaped at her with goggling eyes, for she laughed, a clear, silver peal of mocking music. She had a wide-mouthed, boyish face, tanned, glowing with health. I saw full lips, voluptuously crimson, flashing eyes under arched, sardonic brows, and a full-breasted, wasp-waisted figure that moved with seductive grace and Amazonian vigor.

Then my weary, drugged mind could cling to consciousness no more, and darkness rose to drown me.

When I awoke, the succulent odor of roasting meat was thick in my nostrils and the din of strange twanging music, mingled with the casual laughter of men, was in my ears. I lay in warm softness, drinking in the mouth-watering smell of hot food, dreamily thinking of nothing, until someone said, quite close to me, "He has awakened. Call Siona!"

I opened my eyes and looked around me. All was gloom and shadow, struck through with wavering orange firelight, and for a moment I thought it must be night. But—no—that could hardly be, for our struggle with the vampire blossom had been in early morning and I could hardly have slept for so many hours as to awake after sunfall.

Looking about, I saw we were enclosed on all sides by a rough dark surface. A—cave? Surely that could not be! Then I saw the roughness was that of wood, and I realized we were within the trunk of a hollow tree, or a hollowed-out portion of a tree. A cheery fire blazed amidst the tree cave, painting monstrous black shadows over the uneven walls. Perhaps twenty men and boys sat or sprawled around the blaze, some drinking from cups that looked like halves of hollowed, enormous acorns; others strummed on musical instruments that resembled mandolins or Medieval viols. Turning on a wooden spit over the crackling fire, meat was roasting, fat dripping into the flames.

By my side, eyes enormous in her pale, heart-shaped face, Niamh sat with her back against the wooden wall, staring into the flames. She looked pale and exhausted, and was doubtless weak from loss of blood, but she was alive and did not seem to have taken harm from her horrible experience.

"Who are these people who have rescued us, Niamh?" I asked in a low voice.

"Outlaws and bandits of the forest," she said. "Exiles, fled from justice . . . oh, I fear we have but fallen into a greater danger, having come into their hands!"

"Why do you say that?" I asked. "They are friendly, or they would not have saved us from that terrible flower. . . ."

She shuddered at the memory of the experience.

"They know no law but their own, and every man's hand is against them, even as their hand is turned against every man. I fear they saved our lives for some reason of their own! Ransom, perhaps, or . . . even worse."

"Slavery?" I hazarded.

She shook her head reluctantly. "They live in lawless freedom, bandit warriors equal each to the other, under an elective chieftain—in the case of this band, that strange woman, Siona—'the Huntress,' they call her. *Oh!*"

Her eyes widened. I looked up into the grinning face of the strange outlaw girl whose face had been the last thing I had seen before I fell unconscious. Lithely she stood, legs spread in boyish stance, head on one side, regarding us with bright-eyed curiosity, the slim, tanned fingers of one strong, capable little hand toying with the pommel of a dagger.

"Aye, mistress, 'the Huntress,' my men call me," the woman said in a clear bell-like voice in which overtones of sleek, cat-like mockery were audible. "And what shall I call you, whom I plucked from the bosom of the blood-drinking flower?—'the Quarry'?"

Her mocking gaze fell on me, and her expression sharpened with reluctant admiration, measuring my inches, lingering on my flat belly, deep chest, broad shoulders.

"And what of you, my lusty lad? You have the girth of a gladiator, the arms of a wrestler. Ah! I have it—'the Champion,' eh?" She laughed throatily, revealing small, even teeth, startlingly white against the bronze tan of her features.

"We are harmless travelers, nothing more," said Niamh in a toneless, controlled voic.

"Perhaps," Siona purred. "And yet—'tis curious, you'll admit—unarmed, lone travelers seldom venture into the middle terraces, preferring the upper tier and the great cities. Your champion has the look of a woodsman about him, but not you, my dainty lady! I'll warrant those soft legs are more used to velvet skirts and silken couches than to scrambling about the giant boughs. And where are you bound, unarmed and unmounted, you travelers?"

"To the city of Phaolon," murmured Niamh. I kept my mouth shut, sensing that she had more insight into this situation and its hazards than had I.

"Phaolon, is it? In truth, you choose an awkward route, and will find the road difficult, without a *dhua!* And I wonder what purpose you have, ragged travelers, in seeking the Jewel City alone and afoot? The wild is a savage realm, and the great trees conceal a thousand horrors which lie in wait for the unwary. To venture forth into such peril argues an overwhelming cause. . . ."

"We are from the city of Kamadhong," Niamh said with a glibness that won my admiration. "We did not flee into the wild from free choice, but to avoid persecution. We make for the Jewel City of Phaolon for 'tis said the queen of that realm offers a haven to all who come to her in need."

The Huntress frowned, pouting her ripe red mouth.

"A haven, is it? Well, mayhap: but the outlaws of the

wild have never found a gracious host in her who holds the gold throne of Phaolon. In truth, her chevaliers hunt us as they will, as if we were but savage beasts, not men!"

At this candid appraisal, Niamh bit her lip, flushing, and bent her head. But the wild outlaw girl did not seem to notice.

"But, now—your story interests me, girl! 'Persecution,' you said it was you fled from. Tell me of that—what manner of persecution do they practice in Kamadhong against dainty ladies and their stalwart champions?"

Again, Niamh glibly concocted a reasonable story to account for our fictitious flight from a city of which I had never heard.

"We are the children of rival houses," she said firmly, "and we—we would wed against the wishes of our houses. I am of an ancient family of the *thurkūz*, and my lover is a mighty warrior of the *khaweng-ya*, whose love is deemed beneath one of my rank."

Now it was my turn to flush and fidget, but again the Amazon girl did not appear to notice the involuntary reaction.

The story which the princess had invented on the spur of the moment to account for our being found alone and unarmed, wandering amidst the branches of the colossal trees, was, actually, a good one which made perfect sense. I have mentioned before something of the system of hereditary castes into which the civilization of the Laonese is divided. To Siona, it would be quite logical that a daughter of the *thurkūz*, the landed and titled aristocracy, should be forbidden to wed a soldier of the lowly warrior class, the *khaweng-ya*.

In truth, she did not even question it. She eyed me with a bold and almost flirtatious appraisal, and said: "I can understand your reluctance to yield to the wishes of your family in such a matter, girl. If I had a lover with such shoulders, I, too, would cling to him!"

She shrugged, dismissing the matter.

"Well, you are welcome here, for this band does truly offer a haven to the homeless and the outcast! Take your place at the cook-fire; eat and drink your fill. With sunfall we depart for a place of greater safety, and you may come with us, if such be your wish, for our path tends in the direction of the city that is your goal and we have *zaiph* to spare, having lost three of our number to the

hazards of the chase during this hunting expedition. Rest
well—we depart ere long!"

And with those words, and a casual flip of her hand, the
outlaw girl turned on her heel and strode off. Niamh
sagged with relief and smiled weakly at me. It was dangerous for us to speak, not knowing what ears might be
listening, so I postponed to another time the questions that
seethed within me. I assumed it was a mere instinct of
caution that had bidden Niamh to conceal her identity and
my own from Siona, and to invent a spurious account of
our being here in place of the true story.

We joined the ring about the fire and feasted heartily on
a venison-like meat, coarse black bread, and segments of
fresh fruit, washed down with fierce red wine. The foresters welcomed us among them, studiously avoiding questions; their rude and careless hospitality was welcome, and
I gathered that it was not unheard-of for strangers to join
their band for a meal. Many of them were branded
outlaws, but they did not seem a depraved or vicious lot,
although they were a hard-faced crew, their tongues full
of strange oaths, and very ready to brawl.

Considering the casual, offhand welcome they gave us,
and their lack of curiosity toward us, I wondered that
Niamh kept her head bent, her face in shadow as much as
possible, and spoke little. But I could hardly ask her
reasons.

Chapter 14

OUTLAWS' LAIR

When we at last left our temporary haven in the hollow branch, the heavens were ablaze with the green-gold sunset that made the forest world so strange. Shafts of unearthly molten jade sunlight fell through the monstrous branches; gloom gathered, concealing with its velvet shadow the sunny, open vistas that had stretched to all sides with day.

We were placed in the care of a sturdy rogue called Yurgon, who seemed to function as one of Siona's underchiefs or squad lieutenants. From the brisk efficiency wherewith the departure was undertaken, I saw much in the outlaw band to admire. Among the Laonese I had known at Niamh's palace, there were few like these hardy woodsmen. Only my faithful Panthon and a few of the guards in my entourage could match these strong, lean, silent, manly huntsmen, for, by and large, the male Laonese of my acquaintance had been slender, frail, foppish, and of a delicately effeminate beauty.

But the outlaws of Siona's band were men through and through, and knew the meaning of discipline. In a trice the *zaiph* were saddled and ready, the outlaws mounted, the saddlebags containing the kills made on the hunt securely lashed to the baggage-*zaiph,* and all was ready.

Siona lifted her curved hunting horn and sounded a clear, imperious call. Squad by squad, in perfect order, the outlaws rose from the enormous bough. Wings drumming, the *zaiph* formed a double line with Siona's mount to the fore, and hurtled up a long slanting ray of fading sunlight into the upper terraces of the giant forest. Darkness fell swiftly.

I wondered at the wisdom of traveling by night, which seemed to my thought far more dangerous than traveling by day. For one thing, the more dangerous predators were aprowl during the reign of darkness, and, as well, in the gloom that shrouded the world of giant trees after sunfall, traveling should be much more difficult, for it was easier to miss your landmarks and go astray. Summoning my courage, I asked Yurgon of this, since he rode to my right hand.

He shrugged. "There is little danger, Champion. The beasts avoid *zaiph* for they find them scrawny and their meager flesh unappetizing. And we are in little danger of straying from our route—see yonder gleam of light?"

He pointed to a smudge of greenish luminescence so faint I would not have noticed it had he not pointed it out to me. It was a dull glimmer of phosphorescence, scarcely visible amidst the gloom. I nodded, and asked him what it was.

"The slime exhuded by the *phuol*," he said, naming a repugnant form of giant insect life which resembled the scorpion. "By day the slime is not visible; by night it sheds a pallid glow, wherewith our scouts have blazed a trail through the giant trees."

"Very well," I said. "But I still fail to see why you outlaws prefer to travel by night rather than by day, since you are in little danger from predators in any case."

He gave a harsh laugh and for a moment his frank face was cruel. "The most dangerous of all predators is man himself," he said. "And it is from our fellow men that our greatest perils come. For we of the woods, who prefer the freedom of the trees to the safety of cities, are deemed the enemy of every city man. In truth, the hand of every man is against us—the knights of Phaolon, in particular, hunt us like beasts and slay us when they can. But when the darkness reigns, the city dwellers fear to fly abroad, lest they lose themselves in the black of night."

I was glad it was so dark that Yurgon could not see the expression on my face at his words. Now I knew why the princess had concealed her identity behind a mask of subterfuge, and why she had hidden her face as best she might!

We flew on for an hour or more. It would be mean-
ingless to say that I became completely lost, because I had
been thoroughly lost when the outlaws first rescued us
from the vampire blossom. But I noticed that flight became slower and more difficult, that the web of interlac-
ing branchlets tightened around us, and that screens of
leaves blocked our path with ever-increasing frequency,
until drawn aside by cunningly-concealed ropes.

We reached at last the secret city of the outlaws—if
"city" is not too grandiose a word whereby to describe a
huddle of huts in the crotch of a mighty bough, hung
about almost entirely with immense clumps of golden
leafage which most effectively screened from view the lair
of the bandit clan. The site had obviously been selected
for its solitude and remoteness, and as much as for its lack
of visibility, which last feature, I later learned, had been
considerably enhanced by art. For wherever nature had
carelessly left open a vista through the screening leaves,
the outlaws had with cunning artifice arranged to block
the opening. Branchlets had been twisted awry, tied into
position with stout thongs, and, with time, had grown into
their new position.

We came to rest in the open space at the center of the
outlaw village and dismounted. All was unbroken gloom;
no slightest chink was left unblocked, to betray the hide-
out of the robber band by a vagrant gleam of light.
Windows were heavily curtained with thick-woven fiber,
or shuttered stoutly. Siona led us into the central structure
of the encampment; the edifice was many times larger
than the other huts, which were mostly low, hummock-like
excrescences whose bark-and-branch fabric caused them
to blend unobtrusively with the substance of the vast,
gnarled and knotted branch itself.

But this central structure was at least three stories in
height, and was built against the trunk of the tree, following and melting into its curves; thatched roofs artificially
gilded the uniform gold of the living leaves. Even by
daylight, the structure would have been difficult to identify
as the work of human hands. The artisans of Siona's troop
were masters of the difficult and exacting science of
camouflage—but such would only have been natural, I
suppose. Survival depends largely on remaining unseen, or
on becoming difficult to perceive: and the outlaw band
had made of survival a true art.

The barred door was opened by alert guards at Siona's knock; we entered, brushing past permanent light-blocking screens of woven rattan-like reeds or fibers (made, I later learned, from the skeletal structure of leaves), and came into a large, warm hall whose raftered ceiling was lost in flickering shadows.

A broad-lipped fire-well was set in the center of this room, its depth and rondure hewn into the very wood of the branch. This circular pit had been lined with mortared stones, or fragments of stones, in order to render it fireproof, and a glowing bed of coals hissed and simmered therein. Long wooden benches, and low rough-hewn tables, were set in a huge semicircle about this central fire-pit, and there were about two dozen people in the hall as the hunting party entered. Some of these were men, but most of them were women, and there were a few children to be seen.

The outlaw women were a hardy lot, bright-eyed, red-lipped, vivacious, clad in vests and skirts of rude homespun, with many vivid petticoats of gaudy hues. Brilliantly-colored kerchiefs were wound about their heads, and gold bangles glittered at throat and earlobe. They resembled nothing so much as gypsy women, and were a bold-eyed, blatantly flirtatious lot.

As for the men, they were mostly older men, some of them being of quite advanced age, although hale and hearty for all their years. Those among them who were younger seemed largely crippled or injured; I saw one lithe young bandit lacking a leg, and another who wore a scarlet kerchief wound about his brows, obviously to conceal his blindness. These were, I doubt not, the casualties of the outlaw life; and that life, I could well understand, was one filled to the brim with extraordinary perils beyond the casual experience of city dwelling men. The outlaws of the world of giant trees were hunted by the soldiery of every city, and were forced, therefore, to battle for their survival not only against the natural hazards of life in the forest—which crawled with monsters and ferocious predators beyond name or number—but against their fellow men, as well.

The returning huntsmen were greeted with loud cordiality. The fire was stirred and fed until orange flames leaped high, casting vast, writhing shadows across the walls. Women greeted their men with shrieks and laughter and warm embraces; bright-eyed, mischievous-looking ragged children ran squealing underfoot. Skins of wine were fetched from storerooms and were emptied into capacious goblets of glossy wood.

Niamh and I were neither ignored nor made the object of unwelcome curiosity; our presence was taken for granted. Doubtless, many such forays into the outer world resulted in the discovery of wandering exiles, a steady source of new recruits for the outlaw band. Cups of wine were passed to us and a place was made for us at the circular benches which encircled the roaring fire. I took a hearty swallow of the dark, foaming beverage—expecting a suave, mellow vintage such as that to which I had by now become accustomed from my days at the court of Phaolon the Jewel City. Instead, the raw, fiery liquor seared the lining of my throat and brought tears to my eyes; the outlaws had, it seemed, long since discovered the secret of fermentation, and what I had casually mistaken for wine was actually a fierce and very potent brandy!

The weary huntsmen threw themselves down on the benches, hugging and kissing their women, while children ran shrieking to fetch more skins of brandy. A sudden mood of carnival whipped the women into a frenzied gaiety: crude musical instruments were produced from voluminous skirts—music filled the firelit hall with its jangling rhythms—the younger women sprang into a wild dance like a fandango, scarlet petticoats swirling high, revealing tan sinewy thighs and long bare legs.

Raucous toasts were called out. Hoarse, bawdy jests were roared over the crashing music. White teeth flashed in swarthy, laughing faces. The fume of brandy, the heady beat of the wild music, the whirling sinuous forms whipping past in the furious dance, the broiling heat of the crackling bonfire—all these combined to make me suddenly very, very weary.

Yurgon had been keeping an eye on us, as soon became obvious. As I stifled back the third yawn he appeared before us as suddenly as an apparition, gesturing toward a cubicle across the hall which had been designated as ours.

"The night is well advanced," he grinned, "and dawn is near. Come!" He led us through the dancers to our cubicle; and the first difficulty engendered by our false story presented itself: the cubicle had only one—bed!

Niamh blushed and her eyes avoided mine. Yurgon's

keen eye noted this. Tucking his thumbs in his girdle, he
threw his head back and boomed with laughter.

"Such modesty in lovers must be rare!" he chuckled.
"Come, we have no priests here—'tis time the blush of
modest maidenhood were changed to lovers' eager glow!"
With a wink he turned on his heel and left us to our own
devices.

I set my jaw resolutely. There was nothing else to do
but to see it through. It would never do to cast our story
into suspicion by a reluctance to share the same bed. I
muttered as much to Niamh, and she clambered into the
dark, stuffy little closet-like cubicle and sank into the
remotest possible corner of the mattress, while I climbed
in, jamming myself as close to the doorway as possible.

Very little privacy was possible to us under such
cramped conditions, but at least there was a rough-woven
hanging we could pull across the entranceway to our
narrow little closet. And so we settled down to get what
sleep we could, gingerly avoiding the slightest touch. We
did not, of course, disrobe but slept in our clothing. I lay
there in the stuffy darkness, listening to the uproar, the
shouting, the music of the dance, achingly aware in every
fiber of the nearness of Niamh's body and the rhythm of
her breathing. I did not sleep very well that night.

Chapter 15

I MAKE AN ENEMY

The rustle of curtains drawn suddenly aside awakened me. I was aware of a warm pressure against my shoulder and side, and, turning my head slightly, I saw Niamh nestling against me. During the night she had rolled over in her sleep until now she lay cuddled in the curve of my arm, her cheek pillowed against my breast, one arm flung carelessly about my neck, her slender leg thrown over mine. I felt acutely embarrassed; yet, at the same time, my heart thudded breathlessly against my ribs and I savored the delicious excitement of her nearness and the warm pressure of her body against my own. She slept on, oblivious to the compromising position of intimacy into which her unconscious movements during slumber had placed us.

A throaty chuckle roused me from my dreamful contemplation of her tousled, drowsy loveliness. It was a nasty, suggestive snigger, and I looked about to discover its origin. And found it, to my instant displeasure.

Someone had drawn aside the curtains that screened our sleeping cubicle, and he stood at the entrance peering in. I recognized him at a glance. It was one of the huntsmen from the night before, a member of the party which had rescued Niamh and myself from the murderous embrace of the vampire blossom. I could not at once recall his name, although I soon learned that he was called Sligon. He was a little man with a twisted back, long, dangling, anthropoid arms, and something wrong with one leg so that he limped with a peculiar sidling gait like a crab.

He had a swarthy, ugly face with hot, leering eyes and his face habitually wore a sort of oily, knowing smirk. Among the tall, lean, manly foresters of Siona's band, the hunched, sidling little man stood out very noticeably, which is why I remembered his face although we had never yet exchanged a word.

Now he stood in the entrance of our cubicle, peering in with a gloating smirk on his repellent visage. Doubtless he had been sent to arouse us for the morning meal; however, I did not like the secretive, furtive manner in which he performed his duty. And anger awoke within me at the way he stood leering in on our privacy, running his eyes over Niamh's sleeping loveliness and her long bare legs, his gaze lingering on the glimpses of creamy flesh which showed through the rents and tears in her abbreviated garments. So I kicked him in the face!

The action was a purely instinctive one, performed without forethought, a mere lashing out at something which annoyed me. I had not really meant to kick him at all, just to shove him away, and had my hands been free at the moment, I would doubtless have used them. But they were not, and hence it was my foot that went crashing into his ugly, smirking visage and sent him sprawling.

A roar of amusement rang out as the hunched, sidling little thief crashed, squalling, into the tables. He was on his feet in an instant, eyes agleam with malice, a wicked hooked knife clutched in one hand. He snarled, spitting curses, face vicious, for all the world like a cat dunked suddenly in cold water.

I sprang from the bed as he lunged at me, the knife blade flashing in his hand. On Earth my knowledge of the tricks of rough-and-tumble fighting had necessarily been limited to what I had read in books or watched on television; but the body of Lord Chong knew all about gutter brawls, and instinctive habit patterns snapped into action.

I knocked his knife-hand aside, blocking his lunge with the blunt edge of my forearm, and sank my balled fist into his abdomen. The breath whistled from between his yellow snagged teeth. His face paled to a sickly hue and he sank to his knees and crouched there, gagging and sucking for breath. The fight had suddenly gone out of him from that one blow of mine, and as I bent to pick up the wicked little knife that he had let fall from numb, nerveless fingers paralyzed by my blocking blow, I reflected yet again on the obvious benefits of possessing the body of a fighting man, a body with superbly trained, hair-trigger reflexes!

In the next instant, burly Yurgon stepped between us, plucking Sligon from the ground by the scruff of his neck and shoving him away, turning stern eyes on me—stern, that is, if you discounted the appreciative grin that tugged at the corners of his mouth.

"No fighting, you two!" he snapped. "Siona's rule—any further trouble between the two of you and I'll have you both flogged. Is that understood?"

I nodded. "Perfectly! But it should also be understood that if yonder fellow or anyone else comes slinking around to peer through the curtains at the prin—at my mate and myself—he will get another boot in the teeth, flogging or no flogging. I hope *that* is understood!"

Yurgon chuckled. "Aye, Champion! Sligon, you sneak, stay away from our guests from now on, or I'll give you the boot myself, understand?"

The little weasel of a man nodded silently, eyes vicious, saying nothing. I tossed him his knife and turned on my heel to where Niamh crouched in the doorway of the sleeping cubicle, flushed and bewildered, not understanding the reason for this altercation.

I assumed the incident was closed, and put it out of my mind. But as the little thief turned to slink away, he shot one glance at me from scowling eyes. It was a shaft of pure scarlet hatred, that glance, and I would have done well not to have discounted it. However, I paid it and him no particular heed, and therein, as shall ere long be seen, lay my downfall and Niamh's doom. On such slight accidents do the hinges of destiny turn.

Siona, who slept with the unwed women in another part of the keep, had missed the altercation and no one bothered to inform her of it. When she appeared for the morning meal she noticed the sorry condition of our garments, which by now had been reduced to mere rags hardly sufficient to conceal our modesty, and curtly bade one of the foresters to find us more fitting raiment.

After breakfast, the huntsman commanded to this duty

conducted us to the storerooms and saw us outfitted properly.

The fellow in question, by the way, was a fresh-faced, eager young lad named Kaorn, who seemed to be about sixteen or seventeen as far as I could judge—which was not very far, as the age of the Laonese people and their average life span remains something of a mystery to me to this very hour. I have not yet had occasion to touch upon the mystery of time on the World of the Green Star thus far in the course of this narrative, but if my reader will permit a slight digression at this point, while Niamh and I are getting dressed, I will mention that there was something peculiar and extraordinary about time on this planet.

The passage of time went largely unmarked among the Laonese, and even in their conversation they hardly ever referred to it. Among my own people, it is very common to employ such words as day and night, hour and minute—all of which, of course, refer to minor time divisions commonly, indeed universally, understood. "I'll be there in ten minutes," we are accustomed to saying; or "I spoke to him only an hour ago," or "I called him last week." Virtually every action and activity undertaken by us in our everyday lives is performed against, or rather within, a framework of reference to time.

This is, most mysteriously, not at all the case with the slender, ivory-skinned inhabitants of the World of the Green Star. Such familiar time references are almost wholly absent from their speech as from their way of thinking, although this fact is not at once noticeable and took me quite some time to become aware of. When I did begin to notice it I believe I put it down to two facts. The first of these facts is that the Laonese people are of a pre-industrial civilization which has not yet reached the level of technology appropriate to the invention of clocks. Without possessing clocks, or some kind of device to measure the passage of time, it is understandable that references to hours and minutes would be highly arbitrary and unlikely—a fact generally overlooked by the authors of popular historical novels.

The second fact is, simply, that the Laonese rarely observe their sun. Both their sun and the various stars and constellations are generally hidden behind the dome of pearly mists that veil the heavens from their view as effectively as if they were inhabitants of the planet Venus. On Earth, of course, the sun is continuously visible throughout the daylight hours, and its passage from dawn to dusk easily observed. But the Green Star that is the sun of this world can scarcely be seen through the clouds that cover the skies, and although it is even then dimly visible as a center of brightness, the heavy leafage and immense branches wherein the folk of this world commonly dwell further obscure their notice of it.

But above and beyond the fact that the Laonese seldom refer to time by its subtler divisions—their language lacking even the words for hour or minute—they make no reference to the seasons of the year, and seldom refer even to the passage of the years. Unfortunately, my stay on the World of the Green Star was far too brief for me to have observed the passage of the seasons, but it may well have been that this planet is not so severely inclined upon its axis for the differences in temperature between the seasons to be particularly noticeable. I am left with the feeling that the Laonese dwell in a world of perpetual summer, verging, it may be, on the beginnings of autumn.

At any rate, during the time I lived among them, the Laonese seldom referred to years in any sense and for any purpose. I believe that I have already mentioned how difficult it was to estimate the age of some of the individuals whom I encountered during my stay on this strange and alien planet. Khin-nom, the old sage of Niamh's court who taught me the language spoken by the Laonese, was an example of this. He was clearly a man of more than mature years, lean and gaunt and bewhiskered, his keen eyes and measured tones indicative of long experience and deep thought. But I would be at a loss to guess his age, for the flesh of his face was firm and healthy and unlined, his step vigorous and not in the least halting, and his body preserved the elasticity and suppleness of youth.

I wonder if it is due to the fact that their sun is not easily visible and that the giant trees about them show little change with the passage of the seasons, that the Laonese have no clearly formed conception of time, never think about it, and thus, not being aware of the passing of years, remain somehow oblivious to the effects of age? Is it possible that if a person is oblivious to the passing of years he retains the health and vigor of his youth even into well-advanced old age? Is it possible that for a mind totally ignorant of time to enjoy something closely resembling perpetual youth?

I do not know; I cannot say. This is a question for the philosophers to ponder over, and I am a man of action, not a philosopher.

Before long young Kaorn had us outfitted in the garb of the forest outlaws. I was given a supple, thigh-length tunic of some soft leathery stuff with a nap on it like suede, together with short boots, a heavy leathern girdle, short cloak, and leggings. Niamh reappeared looking for all the world like Maid Marian in a Robin Hood movie, with an abbreviated and tight-fitting jupon of forest green, soft high-laced buskins, and a feathered cap which perched winsomely atop her silken mane. She looked completely adorable, although I was too tongue-tied to say so. Kaorn, less inhibited than I, grinned in appreciation, eyes shining with boyish adoration. Niamh dimpled at the expression on the boy's face as she pirouetted before us in her new raiment.

We rejoined the others, and, looking about, I spotted Sligon at a far corner of the hall, huddled spitefully on the end of a bench, pointedly ignoring us. My flash of temper had long since subsided and I would willingly have healed the breach between the little thief and myself, but beyond shooting me one vicious glare, he ignored me therewith, turning his back on me, and it would have been awkward for me to have made any friendly overture.

Obviously, he nursed a grudge against me. With a slight sinking feeling, I realized that I had made an enemy.

An enemy who would neither forget—nor forgive.

Part IV

THE BOOK OF SLIGON
THE BETRAYER

Chapter 16

THE SECRET OF SIONA

Our position among the outlaws of Siona's band was anomalous and never quite defined. We were not exactly captives, for we were permitted considerable freedom of movement and there were but few overt strictures placed on our conversation, our behavior, or our whereabouts. Nor were we precisely guests, for both of us were expected to shoulder our share of the work, Niamh the household tasks and myself guard duty and weapons practice, and we were both under the orders of our squad leader, Siona's lieutenant, Yurgon. On the other hand, we could hardly be considered as new recruits, since we had neither volunteered to join the band of foresters nor had we been invited to do so.

For the time being, it seemed simplest to merely do as

we were bidden without asking questions, voicing protests, or in any way drawing undue attention to ourselves. The question of our being permitted to continue on our way to Phaolon simply did not arise for discussion. Certainly, without active assistance of the outlaws it would have been impossible for us to do so, although it occurred to me several times that we could easily have escaped from the outlaw stronghold any time we wished, since we were never under guard at any given occasion and could move about as we wished.

I don't know whether Yurgon and his fellows considered us to be prisoners or what, but there was certainly no need for him to place a guard over us. We had not the slightest idea of our whereabouts, nor in which direction lay the Jewel City that was our goal, and without information or the help of the outlaws we could not have traveled the distance and would have been completely lost in moments, had we been so foolish as to make the attempt unaided.

I did not mind the tasks assigned to me, for my muscular body demanded exercise and I was eager to continue learning the use of the Laonese weapons. A brief tour of guard duty every night or so was no great burden and I rather enjoyed the rough, manly camaraderie of the guards, so very different from the languid and effete relationships I had known at the court of the Princess of Phaolon. There, but for the sturdy fellowship I had enjoyed with my brave, loyal Panthon and the other guards assigned to my entourage, I had known nothing like this rough and ready masculine comradeship.

For Niamh, however, the life we shared with the outlaws of Siona's band must have been very trying, although to give the gallant princess credit where credit is due, she allowed no word of complaint to escape her lips. Siona had, I think quite naturally, assigned the princess household duties such as were shared by the unmarried or underage women of the encampment. It was her task to keep the fires going, to share in cooking the meals and in serving them, and to clean the kitchen and the eating implements after their use.

Frankly, I thought little of this. It did not for any reason occur to me that Niamh was being singled out for rough or dirty or degrading work, since the same tasks were the common lot of the other women who worked cheerfully at her side. However, the delicately reared princess had never been accustomed to performing even the slightest household labor, having been reared in conditions of the greatest luxury, surrounded by maids and servants of every description, and the simple tasks that now fell to her lot must have been a bothersome burden to her. Doubtless she had little in common with the bold-eyed kitchen girls and it was not long before they sensed this from her queenly reserve and the maidenly reticence of her speech, which was very unlike the crude and bawdy language they employed, spiced with oaths and flavored with rude jests.

At any rate, even I, in my ignorance, soon became aware of a change in the way in which Niamh was being treated by the wenches—despite the fact that she never gave voice to a word of complaint when she was with me.

In particular, I noticed that she no longer ate with me during the daylight meals, and instead had become one of the serving girls who tended the tables. This did not seem to me to be worthy of comment, for without thinking much about it I naturally assumed that the kitchen girls were assigned to wait on tables according to some sort of rotation system. But she continued in this role and it soon became obvious to me that the task had been made hers in punishment.

I first became really aware of this when I noticed that she was exclusively waiting on Siona during these meals, and that the huntress more than once spoke sharply to her, upbraiding her for some clumsiness, either actual or fancied. These scoldings were loudly performed before the full company in such a way as to degrade and shame her even before the other kitchen women. And it shortly became obvious that Siona was going out of her way to mistreat and insult the dainty Princess of the Jewel City.

One evening in particular stands out in my memory. Niamh had been at work for many hours at the hot and wearisome task of turning the spit upon which our dinner meat was cooked over a slow fire. This singularly disagreeable task was generally reserved for those girls who had misbehaved in some manner and were being punished for their lapse. As the meats dripped continually into the spluttering fire, the girl assigned to tend the spit became

splattered with grease from head to foot in no time, and
Niamh was no exception to this.

While serving wine at Siona's peremptory command, the
wine beaker had slipped in Niamh's greasy fingers, spilling
purple liquid over Siona's finery. Shrieking a particularly
vile name, the Amazon girl sprang to her face, dealing
Niamh a buffet on the cheek that sent her sprawling.

The wine beaker went flying, smashing to a thousand
ringing shards on the wooden floor, which further enraged
the huntress. She snatched a coiled whip from her ornate
girdle and sent its lash singing about the slender shoulders
of the hapless Niamh.

I leaped to my feet, almost overturning the bench, and
was upon the raised dais where Siona was accustomed to
dine alone in a single bound. Without pausing to consider the possible consequences, I caught Siona's wrist in a
crushing grip and tore the whip handle from her, flinging
it away.

The outlaw girl stood, her breasts rising and falling in
their cups of silver openwork filigree as she panted, cheeks
flushing and eyes sparkling with rage. At her feet
crouched the frightened and cowering Niamh amidst a
litter of crystal shards, in a puddle of spreading wine. Her
creamy shoulders were bare and a crimson stripe ran
obscenely across them from the biting kiss of Siona's
whip. Neither of us spoke for a long, frozen moment, and
the hall itself was silent, the rows of foresters staring at
this tableau in tongueless astonishment.

Slowly I relaxed my fingers, freeing Siona's hand. I was
breathing heavily, my eyes misted with fury, and in my
present state I did not trust myself to speak.

Siona's glorious eyes narrowed to slits of cold, burning
rage. Her voice became a sibilant hiss as she cursed me.

"If ever again you lay your clumsy paws on me, you
stinking *ulphio,* I will have you and this bungling, cringing
slut flogged until your backs are reduced to ribbons," she
said venomously.

I should perhaps add that an *ulphio* is a tree scavenger
of singularly loathsome dietary habits and particularly
repulsive appearance—the Laonese equivalent of a rat,
you might say—and its name is commonly employed in
invective to the same purpose.

I said nothing, but stood facing her calmly, my arms
folded now upon my chest. Niamh, however, got silently

to her feet and without so much as exchanging a look with the enraged outlaw queen went into the kitchens, from which ere long she returned with damp rags to begin cleaning up the spilled wine. Still panting with fury, Siona made as if to kick Niamh as she knelt to sponge up the mess. I caught her by the elbow and spun her off-balance so that the blow did not land.

The Amazon girl laid one trembling hand on the arm of her chair and looked at me with eyes like daggers.

"You dare to touch me!" she shrilled.

"I am a guest in your hall," I said calmly, "as is my mate. However, should you ever again attempt to strike my mate for any reason, not only will I touch you, but I will take yonder whip to your back, as you sought to employ it on hers."

Siona's rage was amazing to see. Her beautiful eyes widened to wells of flame; her tanned face whitened, paling to the color of milk; she sank her white teeth in the ripe flesh of her full lips in the fury of her vexation, and dealt me a stinging slap across the mouth. It was not the dainty blow of an ineffectual girl, but a staggering buffet, delivered with all the sinewy strength of her strong young arm, and had I not been braced to receive it I might have been knocked back against the table. As it was, my ears rang and my face went numb, and, although I did not notice it at the time, the rings on Siona's hand cut my lip and blood dribbled down my face.

"You—you—*ulphio!*" she spat.

"*Ulphio* or not," I replied evenly, "I am a guest in your hall. And if this is to be an example of the hospitality you deal to your guests, I begin to think my mate and I might prefer the embrace of the devil flower from which, and perhaps unwisely, you saw fit to rescue us!"

A point touched the naked flesh of my side gently. The cold kiss of the transparent metal awoke me suddenly to the very great danger in which Niamh and I now stood. The beautiful, tempestuous young woman whose eyes blazed into mine in her towering fury was the absolute mistress of this band of cutthroats and condemned outlaws, and our lives at that moment perhaps hung on a slender thread. For Siona was perfectly capable of having both of us whipped—or slain out of hand—or of having us thrust out into the wilderness from which she had rescued us, which would doubtless have the same result as

if she had slain us. There was, however, no way in which I
could have acted differently under such circumstances and
have retained my honor as a warrior and as a man. And
on the whole I believe I had acted with admirable re-
straint under such extreme provocation.

Yurgon cleared his throat before Siona could speak
again. He stood at my shoulder, the tip of his shortsword—
a weapon not unlike the old Roman *gladius*—just grazing
my ribs.

"Guest-right is guest-right," he observed in a soothing
tone, clearly audible the length of the hall. "An apology
might perhaps serve to cool all tempers. . . ."

Siona's ripe lips writhed in a silent snarl; suddenly, and
inexplicably, her eyes welled brimful of tears and her face
crimsoned in a flaming blush. Without a further word, her
eyes failing to meet mine, she turned and left the hall, and
did not reappear again that evening.

Tension relaxed visibly. A few men chuckled under
their breath and one or two expelled long-pent breaths in
a deep sigh of relief. Yurgon grinned, put away his sword,
and made a gesture as of wiping his brow.

"You were near death at that moment, friend," he
muttered with a smile.

"I do not doubt it," I said. "And I will try to see that
such an outburst does not again occur."

He nodded and clapped me on the shoulder.

"It would be wise of you to do that," he agreed; and we
returned to complete our interrupted meal. The meats had
grown cold and the wine had gone lukewarm, but my
appetite had vanished anyway. I drank and chewed automatically, wondering again and again the reason for
Siona's inexplicable dislike and persecution of my beloved,
and why her temper should have blazed up at me.

The secret of her behavior did not at once become
apparent. To me, at least. I doubt not, in cool hindsight,
but that everyone else in the hall knew the secret of Siona
of which I, in my masculine obtuseness, remained ignorant.

Chapter 17

A KNIFE IN THE DARK

Sligon had, of course, been a witness to that dramatic scene of confrontation during dinner, and as I took my place on the benches at its termination, it did not escape me how much the twisted and spiteful little thief had enjoyed my discomfiture. He writhed about in his place at the far end of the hall, laughing silently, his mean little eyes filled with vengeful glee.

I, of course, ignored his very evident enjoyment of my predicament. It would do Niamh or myself no good at all to further antagonize one of the band who already had cause enough to dislike me. So I generally kept out of his way and I noticed that Sligon avoided my own company as much as was possible.

That night as we retired I questioned Niamh about the incident, but she displayed a curious reticence and was obviously reluctant for some reason to discuss the flare-up of Siona's temper.

We were still forced to sleep in the same bed, maintaining our pretense of being runaway star-crossed lovers, and while this imposed a certain degree of intimacy upon us, I, at least, strove quite manfully to avoid violating her privacy by word or thought or deed. While I was by this time very deeply in love with the Princess of the Jewel City—a fact which I am quite certain she knew—it would not have been gentlemanly or very honorable of me to have taken advantage of the situation in which we found ourselves thrown together in such proximity. For her part, Niamh seemed rather reserved. She seldom spoke to me, save to reply to my own queries politely, and maintained a degree of reserve that grew frostier day by day.

This may have been nothing more than her way of discouraging in advance any attentions I might press upon her. That was my first thought, and I must confess that her behavior irritated me. After all, when a gentleman is very gallantly acting like a gentleman, he deserves at least some credit for his chivalry! But ere long it occurred to me that Niamh's coolness toward me had some inexplicable connection or resonance with Siona's own peculiar behavior—but, for the life of me, I couldn't understand what that connection could be.

Although reluctant to discuss the matter, Niamh did at length respond to my questioning, saying that it was because of Siona's wishes that she had been relegated to the more disagreeable of the kitchen tasks, and also that it was on the express command of the Amazon girl that she was selected to serve her at table. Niamh did not, however, voice any opinion as to the reasons for Siona's dislike of her, which it seemed amounted to something very close to genuine persecution.

"Why in the world has she taken such a dislike to you?" I puzzled aloud that night as we lay side by side, carefully apart in the darkness of our stuffy little sleeping cubicle. "I can't understand why she should want to humiliate you before the eyes of everyone in so blatant a manner."

"Perhaps for contrast," Niamh murmured enigmatically.

"Contrast?" I repeated. There came to my mind a vision of the scene that had transpired that evening in the great, high-raftered hall. Siona, her boyish garments laid by, in a beautiful and rather revealing robe of semitranslucent gauzy stuff, gems flashing at wrist and throat, lobe and brow, silken hair worked up into an elaborate coiffure, her narrow waist cinched in by an ornate girdle of gem-studded plates of precious metal which lent emphasis to the rondure of her breasts and the swelling lines of her hips and thighs—and poor Niamh, with her smudged face and straggling, uncombed hair, grease-stained kirtle done up, serving the outlaw girl with rough, work-reddened hands.

"Contrast? I don't understand what you mean," I confessed in a baffled tone. Niamh gave me a long, cool, faintly amused glance.

"Don't you? No, I can see that you do not," she said. And with that she rolled over, her face turned from me, and fell asleep ... leaving me staring at the ceiling, completely mystified, pondering the inexplicable perversities of the female mind.

Sligon, as I have mentioned, tended to avoid my company insofar as it was possible for him to do so; but this was not always possible, as his tasks occasionally conjoined with mine.

One of the first incidents on which they did so took place, as it happened, only a night later. Yurgon had guard captaincy that next evening, and the members of his squad were set in their posts. Sligon was a member of Yurgon's company, and from the time when she had effected the rescue of Niamh and myself from the deadly embrace of the vampire blossom, Siona had placed me under the authority of Yurgon, an order which she had never bothered to rescind. Thus, in effect, I was of Yurgon's company still, although not a formal member of the outlaw band.

There is no walking of the post when you stand guard in a tree two or three miles high in the air. Guards are mounted in far-spaced lookout stations and there they stay till sunup, or until such time as they are relieved. These lookout stations rather resemble the crow's nests on a ship, being small, cramped platforms fastened to the ends of branches or the heights of the tree. A wicker railing runs around these platforms about waist-high, and the platforms themselves are securely bound to twig or branch with leathern thongs. They are also usually screened from view by the sort of camouflage I described earlier—twigs or branchlets unobtrusively bent awry so that the huge leaves conceal the platform from any casual notice.

The post Yurgon assigned to me on the night following my dramatic confrontation with the enraged Siona was a remote and lofty one, situated high up in the gigantic tree whereupon the outlaw camp was built. You could only get up to it by climbing a sort of rope ladder, and once in it, you were stuck there till either dawn or your relief came, as the rope ladder was untied and carried away. It was known as "red branch station" in the casual slang of the guards, for the branchlet at whose end it was situated was covered with a variety of fungus or mold which was of a

distinctive and unique coloration. When Yurgon read out
my name and station I could not help but notice that
Sligon pricked up his ears. An expression of cunning
passed over his ugly, rat-like face, and a gleam of calcula-
tion flickered momentarily in his narrow eyes, until, as if
by a conscious effort, he wiped his face smooth and
innocent of expression.

At the time, this did not seem to be of any importance
and I ignored it. Later, of course, I recalled it all too well.

The scuffle of something moving on rough bark awoke
me instantly from the light doze into which I had fallen.

Nights on the world of giant trees were of an impenetrable degree of darkness. It was during the hours of night
that the most dread and fearsome of the many predators
of this planet were abroad, and that which hunted generally did so in complete silence so as not to alarm its prey.
So it was that, save for the faint and unending whispering
of breeze through the infinitude of leaves, the nights were
not only utterly black, but of a ghostly silence as well.

Hence, the slightest sound of an unusual nature tended
to arouse suspicion. This is why I snapped to full wakefulness from my dreaming doze when that faint scuffing
sound reached my ears. I was crouched at the bottom of
the high-railed little platform, my knees bent, for the floor
space was miniscule; in an instant I was on my feet,
leaning over the wickerwork railing, straining every sense
to the fullest.

An almost undetectable tremor ran up the tapering
branchlet at whose terminus I was stationed. The vibration
was so slight that I might probably not have noticed it at
all, had I not been roused to full alertness by the scuffling
sound a moment before. I held my breath, heart thumping
against my ribs, wondering what slithering monstrosity
was inching its way up the branch to which I clung. We
were under instructions not to rouse the alarm unless an
enemy force was discovered or we ourselves were under
the attack of some beast. My hand went out to the curved
horn bound to the railing at my side. But still I hesitated—
I waited, straining my ears for a repetition of the slight
sound I had heard—not wishing to play the fool, afraid of
the dark, who gives the alarm at the imagined approach
of some nonexistent peril.

Again, that slight tremor up the branch. I had been

conducted to my station by a rope ladder; this had been a length of thick rope with fat knots tied in it every three feet or so. It had been unfastened and carried off once I had attained the platform, for such was the custom. Therefore, whatever dread *thing* was slithering up the branchlet was clinging to the rough bark itself. In the pitch-dark, my fancy painted a variety of monsters, my favorite among them being an enormous serpent. I could almost see the hideous, slithering shape coiled snakily about the narrow branch, its blunt, wedge-shaped head questing through the blackness for the scent of my flesh. . . .

Was it pure imagination, or did I glimpse the faintest flicker of light below me?

Yes—there it was again! A curious double gleam, like two eyes burning through the dark!

If an enormous snake, or some other night-roaming monster, was approaching my station, there was little enough I could do about it. We guards were equipped with a long, broad-bladed hunting knife whose design was strikingly like that made famous by Colonel Jim Bowie of American frontiersman history: each of us carried one of these all-purpose weapons, which was called a "guard-knife." We also wore, strapped across our shoulders, a spear or javelin about nine feet long; these, however, formed the extent of our weapons, it being the purpose of a guard to look and listen and, when necessary, give the alarm, but not to fight. It occurred to me that I might well be able to dislodge whatever creature clung to the rough bark if I reached down with my spear. The brute was directly below me now; I could hear its breathing.

Quick as thought I reached down, probing with my spear—

Two things happened almost simultaneously.

As I bent down to probe beneath me with the spear, something went hissing past my face. In the blackness I caught only the vaguest glimpse of it as it flew by; but the nights of this planet are not so dark but that a dim ghost of light cannot be mirrored in—the blade of a knife!

At the same moment as the thrown knife went flashing past my head to vanish in the darkness, my spear came into contact with something that clung tenaciously to the bough directly beneath the platform whereon I stood. I jammed the shaft of the spear down between it and the branch and, using all the leverage I had, flung my arms out, effectively dislodging it.

An unearthly yowl sounded and some heavy object went crashing and bumping and blundering down through the foliage to a lower branch.

A moment or so later, Yurgon appeared.

"Red branch station—was it you who cried out?" he called.

"Some night creature approached my position," I said, "but I beat it off."

"Very good! But next time, if you are under attack, sound your horn," he said.

"I doubt if the beast will return," I said innocently.

With dawn we were relieved. Yurgon tossed the coiled rope ladder up to me; I caught it, secured it to the branchlet, and clambered down to join my company. At the tail of the line of guardsmen I glimpsed hunched, limping little Sligon. He had a bruised and battered look to him, and it seemed to me that he limped a bit more painfully than usual.

"Anything to report?" Yurgon inquired.

I shook my head. "Nothing, sir. Did anything else of note occur during the night?"

He shrugged. "Nothing. Sligon was careless enough to lose his guard-knife somehow, but nothing else ... why are you laughing?"

I winked, but did not answer.

Chapter 18

INTIMATIONS OF WAR

Since guards get no sleep during the hours of their duty, save for a harmless bit of dozing, they are generally relieved of all duties for the following day and are permitted to sleep then, if they wish.

Thus, just about the time Niamh was rising, I was going to bed. I told her of the incident of the knife in the dark and how I had managed to pry loose from my branch an unknown creature, which had fallen, squalling loudly, crashing down to thump against the branch below. Shaking with laughter, I also related how poor Sligon had limped so painfully all the way home.

The princess did not seem to find my story very amusing, although she smiled wanly. But her brow soon clouded with worry.

"Should you not tell someone—Yurgon, perhaps? If this goes unreported, will not this Sligon make another attempt on your life?" she asked. I shook my head.

"I do not think so," I said. "I rather imagine little Sligon received punishment enough in his fall. I doubt if he will try the same trick twice in a row; and, anyway, there is little he can do against us. Of course, I shall remain on my guard. The only thing we must be careful about is to see to it that he does not come skulking around spying upon us, for were he to discover that I am the Lord Chong and that you are the Princess Niamh of Phaolon, then he would have an excellent weapon to use against us—"

I broke off suddenly, for just as I had uttered those fateful words a hiss of indrawn breath came to my ears.

117

Had someone been lurking outside our cubicle, listening to our words?

In a flash I drew the curtains aside and sprang out into the hall. But there was no one there; no one at all.

But just vanishing through a doorway I glimpsed a black shape. Was it only my imagination, or did that dark figure have a hunched back and did it walk with the sidling motion of a crab?

The skin prickled at the nape of my neck, under my unshorn warrior's mane. Had the black figure limped painfully on a twisted leg? Had it been Sligon, there, beyond the curtains while we talked? *And had the spiteful little thief overheard when I had been so careless as to utter Niamh's name aloud?*

I stood there helplessly, clenching and unclenching my fists in an agony of indecision, uncertain whether or not I should plunge after that figure, now vanished. Just then my friend Kaorn strode past, yawning sleepily. I grabbed the boy's arm.

"Lad, where is Sligon? Have you seen aught of him?" I demanded urgently.

"Not I," the youth said in a puzzled tone. "He's asleep, I guess—as both you and I should be. Why do you ask?"

"Oh—nothing," I said shortly. Then, clapping him on the shoulder, I returned to my bed.

But I did not sleep. Long after Niamh left to go about her kitchen duties, I tossed and turned restlessly, wondering if it had been Sligon listening beyond the curtain; and, if it had been him, had he heard when I spoke Niamh's name?

Eventually, exhaustion took dominance over my worries, and I slept. But my dreams were dark and troubled ones, nightmares through which a hunched shape shambled monstrously, its leering eyes aflame with a dreadful secret.

Events came to a head that very evening. But first came a surprising event that none of us could have foretold.

While night guards spent their tour perched in tiny crow's nests aloft in the giant trees, Siona's daytime guards combed the vicinity by air, mounted on the beautiful, gigantic dragonflies the Laonese call *zaiph*. Toward late afternoon, one of these far-flung scouts returned with an astonishing message.

During his flight he had observed a party in the black-and-yellow livery of the city of Ardha traveling under a flag of truce. These envoys of Akhmim bore a message from the tyrant-lord of that realm to none other but Siona herself! What this message was, they refused to divulge to any but the girl-leader of the outlaw band, and for this purpose they desired safe-conduct into the very lair of the foresters.

"Admit ambassadors of an enemy kingdom to visit us here in the Secret City?" Siona repeated in tones of amazement and disbelief. "They must be mad to think we would permit them to learn the key of our hiding place!"

"On the other hand," said Yurgon thoughtfully, "it would do no harm to find out what it is they desire of us. They could be carefully blindfolded and flown here by a roundabout route, thus remaining in ignorance of the location of our encampment. . . ."

Siona thought it over, rubbing her small, stubborn chin with thoughtful, musing fingers.

"Well, there is something in what you say. Doubtless there is profit in it, whatever it is the folk of Ardha require of us . . . and it has been too long since you lazy rogues have surprised a merchant caravan out of their gems and plump purses! Yurgon, see to it. I leave the protective measures to your devisal . . . we will meet with these envoys here tonight in the great hall."

Listening at my side, Niamh shivered suddenly, and dug her fingers into the flesh of my arm.

Looking back on the scene from the vantage point of time, I wonder if she had some premonition of the dreadful doom that was about to befall both of us.

Night fell, black as pitch; and it was not until an hour after darkness came down on the World of the Green Star that the envoys of Akhmim of Ardha were conducted into the secret Secret City, as the forest outlaws termed their hidden base.

Yurgon had decided to wait until darkness for added security, for he did not trust the unscrupulous wiles of the Ardhanese envoy. The outlaws were considered the foes of every city, and it was not impossible for a blindfold to slip. But by conducting the party of ambassadors here under cover of night, Yurgon made it doubly certain that the position of the outlaw camp would remain unknown to their yellow-robed enemies.

I felt curiously glad that I had the day off, due to my guard duty the previous night; for thus it would be impossible for Yurgon to have selected me to be one of the guards assigned to accompany the envoys hither by a circuitous route.

Not that it was very likely that any of the envoys could have recognized me—although several high lords of Ardha had accompanied the tyrant-prince to the court of Phaolon on the day of my revivification, and the envoys might just possibly have been among them. At any rate, we all awaited the arrival of the embassy with high curiosity and not a little suspense.

The scene was to be the great hall of the outlaw stronghold. The fire in the circular pit had been heaped high with dry fuel and the flames leaped halfway to the smoke-blackened rafters far overhead, casting a brilliant orange light across the huge room. The tables and benches had been cleared away, and the entire strength of the outlaw band was assembled to hear the words of the envoy. Or *almost* the entire strength, for the clever queen of the foresters did not overlook the possibility of duplicity. A war party might be lying hidden, waiting to follow the blindfolded ambassadors back to the Secret City and take it by surprise. So on this night of nights, Siona had commanded tall, gray-bearded Phryne, who had that night's guard captaincy, to triple his men, employing far-flung and seldom-used stations. And all in the great room had weapons to hand, ready to leap to the defense of their hidden lair should it be attacked.

Siona, decked in war gear, sat on the dais in the great carved throne-like chair that had been her father's. For this rare occasion the Amazon girl wore breast-cups of beaten gold over hard copper, an abbreviated skirt of leather straps studded with small metal plates, and a barbaric headdress of gold and violet plumes. Gold bangles flashed on her strong wrists; gold bands encircled her tanned bare arms; and a gold-hilted dagger was slung about her slim waist. She looked every inch a queen, and I could not help admiring her openly, much to Niamh's obvious annoyance.

As for Siona, she never once looked in my direction. She had avoided the great hall of the stronghold since the night of our argument, and had taken her meals in her own apartments; on the occasions when she could not avoid my company, she had ignored me with a stony reserve that continued to baffle me.

A trumpeter beyond the hall set his horn to his lips and music rang out in a signal that denoted the arrival of the envoys from Ardha. Even now their cockleshell chariot was settling to the level branch before the hall and the gorgeous wings of immense *zaiph* were fluttering to stillness.

The doors were flung open; Yurgon appeared, guiding the blindfolded envoys past the screens and curtains that were erected before the outer door every nightfall, to keep any trace of light from betraying the location of the encampment.

Yurgon led the envoys into the center of the hall until they stood before Siona's throne. Then they were unmasked and their wrists, which had been bound with thongs, were freed. They blinked about them in the orange light—soft, fleshy men with pendulous chins and wobbling paunches, eyes sharp and observant and shrewd in their soft, plump faces. They wore cumbersome robes of yellow cloth adorned with beads of sparkling jet.

Observing Siona seated proudly on her wooden throne, the envoys bowed profoundly in a humble obeisance. The huntress told them to arise and state their business.

"Beauteous and regal lady," began the fattest of the three in an unctuous voice so suave it virtually dripped with oil, "the Great Prince, my master, has bid this lowly one set before you these precious gifts in homage to your legendary loveliness, and in token of our future alliance of mutual profit and assistance."

At his lordly gesture, one of the lesser envoys stepped forward and placed a small chest on the steps which led up to the dais. He bowed himself backward, rejoining his fellows; Yurgon pushed open the casket with the point of his sword and the lid fell backward, revealing a mass of flashing gems that glittered and dazzled in the bold firelight.

"Very pretty," Siona remarked in a cool, disinterested voice. The fat envoy smirked obsequiously.

"In the words of my master, beauty deserves beautiful things," he said.

"The Tyrant of Ardha is noted for many qualities,"

Siona observed, "but generosity is not among them. You spoke of 'future alliance'—hence I must consider these gifts not merely as gifts, but in the nature of payment for some service. What service might that be?"

The envoy beamed. "Beauty, virtue, wit, and intelligence—combined in one!" he enthused. "What penetration! Admirable! Quite admirable!"

"An end to these compliments," the Amazon girl said sharply. "You are here, I take it, to discuss business; very well, then, what business? These trinkets and bright baubles are advance payment for some service; well, what service? Get down to it, man!"

He bowed low.

"As you wish, beauteous lady! Relations have long been strained between the realm of my master and the city of Phaolon. Conditions have deteriorated to the point at which amicable discourse has been severed. The Great Prince has no other recourse for the settling of his grievances but to move in force against the Jewel City—"

Siona straightened, eyes flashing with some strange emotion.

"So that's it," she murmured. "—*War!*"

Standing beside me in the shadows, Niamh sucked in her breath with a gasp and again her fingers tightened upon my arm.

"—*War!*" she echoed in a tense whisper.

Chapter 19

FATE PLAYS A HAND

"*War!*"—the murmur ran through the assembled throng of outlaws like a gust of wind rustling tall grasses. Hands fell to sword-hilts; fingers tightened on pommels.

Siona fixed the Ardhanese envoy with a piercing eye.

"So ... your master—knowing that I have great and good cause to hate and detest the folk of Phaolon, for they thrust my father forth into the wild, in the time of the late prince, father of the present sovereign—thinks to enlist my warriors in his own squabbles, so that my brave foresters can fight and bleed and die to make him regnant over the Jewel City!"

She mused, fingering her mouth. No one spoke. Beside me, Niamh huddled trembling: and I knew now why it was she hid her face from the outlaw queen and concealed her identity with such fearfulness.

The envoy was speaking again.

"The forest outlaws who follow the bold and gallant Lady Siona are masters of the wild and know every path and vantage and vista," he observed. "Keen and clever scouts would they be, in the event of war between the two cities! Of very great cunning are they, wise in the ways of stealth. Unseen, unheard, they move at will through the great trees, and there be none can mark their passing—"

"True," Siona cut in. "The value of my band as scouts of war, however, is many times the sum of these few paltry bangles your master has seen fit to cast at my feet."

"When the Jewel City is taken, will there not be wealth enough for all?" the envoy cried. "The casket is but in the nature of a first payment; there will be many more."

"There will indeed," Siona said decisively, "and the full

124

and total amount agreed on beforehand. But the aerial cavalry of Phaolon is justly renowned in war, and the knights that will rally to the standards of that lady, their queen, are not without bravery. Furthermore, I have heard that a very great warrior has come among them to coach them in the martial arts, a certain Chong. How can Akhmim your master be so confident that from this contest he will emerge the victor?"

The envoy chuckled expansively, jowls jiggling.

"Fate itself has played a hand in deciding the outcome of our strife," he beamed. "The Lord Chong and the Princess Niamh are slain—fallen into the great abyss from a high branch, their very bodies devoured by the beasts— and thus is Phaolon thrown into utter confusion, in lack of a true heir to claim the golden chair of sovereignty. While the wise men and lords of the Jewel City worry and wrangle in their councils, doubt and terror have unmanned the folk of that realm. Now—*now*—is the time to strike, and bear away the victory!"

Siona's eyes flashed; she rose to her feet with a start.

"What is this you say! The hated Niamh dead—am I robbed of my revenge, then, after so long a wait? Is my father's honor not to be avenged at last upon the body of the daughter of his persecutor? Niamh—dead?"

And then it happened.

A shrill, whining voice rose in a shriek of triumphant glee.

"Not so, mistress! Not so at all! For the Lord Chong and the Princess Niamh did not die when they fell into the abyss—indeed, they yet live—*they stand among us now, within this very hall!*"

It was Sligon, of course. The spiteful, ugly little thief sprang upon the dais, gathering all eyes with a dramatic sweep of his arm—then shot his arm out, pointing directly at us where we stood in the shadow of a pillar.

All eyes flew to us. Amazement and wonder and dawning speculation were visible on every face. Yurgon stared at me in blank wonder. Young Kaorn stood bewildered and slack-jawed.

As for Siona, she was transfixed. She stood rigid as if frozen, her face white to the lips, her eyes dead and lusterless. Then they gleamed and there came into her features such an expression of snarling, feline fury and gloating cruelty that I pray I may never again see such an

expression on a human face. The writhing torment of the
Pit glared in her twisted features—and an unholy glee
flamed in her eyes until she no longer resembled anything
human, but looked like a vengeful Fury or some maddened Medusa from the darkest nightmares of elder myth.

I did not wait for her to speak, but flew into action.
There was no chance at all that I could fight my way free
of the hall and escape, bearing away the woman I loved
from the vengeance of Siona. My only hope was to
somehow seize Siona herself, while all stood frozen with
astonishment by this swift turn of events. With my sword-
edge at her throat, it was just barely possible that we
might effect our escape, using her as our hostage.

In one great bound I was on the dais. My hand flew
out, striking the nearest forester to the floor, wrenching
his sword free of its scabbard with a hiss of razory metal
against old leather. But I had not taken the hunched,
sidling little thief into account. For Sligon sprang directly
in my path and stood between Siona and myself. And a
wicked, hooked knife glittered in his hand—the same
knife he had drawn on me once before, when I had
caught him peering into our sleeping cubicle and had
given him a boot in his ugly face by way of reward.

Firelight flashed on knife metal. We engaged our weapons, and such was the fury of his attack that fierce sparks
struck hissing from the clash of blades. A little man with a
hunched back and a twisted leg he might be, but Sligon
knew every vile and despicable trick of gutter fighting, and
he used them all.

Under ordinary circumstances, one armed with a knife
would have but little chance against a man armed with a
sword. But the blade I had seized from the fallen forester
was not the great broadsword wherewith I had trained in
the exercise yards of Phaolon, but a curved, heavy-tipped
cutlass or tulwar—almost a scimitar. It felt clumsy and
poorly balanced and I handled it badly, giving Sligon the
advantage. His blade slid past my awkward guard and I
felt a stinging blow somewhere in my chest. There was
only a moment of pain, and then the sting was replaced by
a cold numbness, so I thought little of the chance blow
and dismissed it as a mere cut, and fought on.

Sligon was not only a cunning and vicious fighter who
knew every dirty trick of infighting ever invented by
human ingenuity, but his warped and twisted little body

concealed a surprising vigor. Deformed his limbs might be, but they possessed a steely strength that was most unexpected. The spiteful little thief was spliced together from whalebone, rawhide and steel wire, and he fought with the fury of thirty devils.

It was his consuming hatred of me that drove him to excel himself. This hatred had rankled and festered at the roots of his soul, devouring him like a canker. How he hurled himself against me, his hooked blade flickering, a blur of brightness in the firelight! It was all I could do to hold my own against him: and a strange weariness was spreading through me, as I grew curiously weaker with every second that passed.

Then came the moment for which Sligon had cleverly waited. My foot edged into a puddle of spilled wine, I lost my balance and fell to my knees. A flash of cruel and gloating glee lit up his slitted eyes. Taking advantage of my momentary inability to defend myself, his blade flashed for my throat as he struck like the loathsome and slinking little coward he was at heart.

One voice soared above the uproar—the clear, silver voice of a woman, hoarsened with emotion—"*No!*"

Then a slim form darted between us. It was Siona, who leaped between the hunched assassin and me like an angry leopardess defending her mate. Sligon paused, his blade hovering, his face transformed from a smirking mask of triumph to blank bewilderment. Then he flinched, grunting. For Siona had driven into his chest the little gold-hilted dagger she wore at her waist; like a striking fang, the slender steel needle had slid into his heart!

Sligon peered down at his breast where a stain of wet crimson spread. His swarthy features paled to the hue of dirty wax. He whimpered, deep in his throat, like a hurt beast. With one hand he pawed at the place where she had hurt him; and then his knees gave way and he fell sprawling on the platform, eyes glazing in death.

So died Sligon the Betrayer, whose treachery had resulted in his own death. . . .

There was no time for me to ponder the implications of Siona's strange and impulsive act. In a flash I had sprung to my feet, seizing her in a strong grip, my blade at her throat. She did not move, did not try to fight my grip or break free, but lay in my arms panting. I turned to face the throng. A score of burly foresters were about to launch themselves upon me.

"If one of you moves, Siona dies," I said grimly. They froze, eyeing me indecisively. My face was a grim mask of determination, my eyes intent and steely. But to this hour I cannot say if I would have actually carried out my threat. I like to think that I would not—after all, Siona had just saved my life, although her actions were surprising and mysterious—and it would not have been in me to have slain a woman, even a woman who was my deadly enemy, and the enemy of the woman I loved.

The foresters and the foreign envoys stood motionlessly. Niamh came quickly through their frozen ranks to my side, her face pale but unafraid. Her slight, girlish bosom rose and fell with her quick breathing, but she seemed composed. She bent and snatched up the hooked knife that Sligon had let fall.

My strange weakness had grown. My arm was like a leaden weight and as I held my blade to Siona's throat my muscles trembled with effort. But there was no time now to think about myself; in the next few moments we would be either safe—or dead.

"We are going out," I said to the room filled with silent men. "Let no one oppose our going, or this blade drinks the life of your mistress. If no one interferes, she will be set free unharmed." There was no answer to this.

"Stay close behind me," I said in low tones to Niamh, "and keep your eyes open. Beware of treachery. . . ."

I shoved the Amazon girl with my arm.

"Move," I said.

We stepped down from the platform whereon the corpse of Sligon lay in a pool of spreading gore. We walked directly for the door of the hall, and as we approached men they stepped aside. My eyes roved constantly from side to side, wary of the slightest move, but not one of the foresters dared to oppose our going with the life of Siona at stake.

Outside, the world was drowned in impenetrable blackness. We found the pens wherein the *zaiph* were stabled, and I told Niamh to single out two steeds for us and to saddle them up. It was a difficult task to perform in such complete blackness, and it must have been doubly hard for her to do it, having never had to saddle her own mount before.

It seemed to take her forever. Siona still had not uttered one word, but stood submissively under my hand. I was watching and listening for some sign of activity in the darkness. There were a thousand small, stealthy sounds in the night, wind among the leaves, the creaking of boughs, the stir and rustling of the *zaiph*. In my fancy I pictured a hundred vengeful foresters creeping upon us under cover of the night. But nothing occurred.

I knew that if we could but mount and fly, no power in the world could take us captive in this impenetrable darkness. The foresters could search all they liked, but we could fly in any direction, to a higher or a lower level, hide in any one of ten thousand places. In the black moonless night we could fly free of pursuit—if only we could make it into the air!

My heart thudding, the taste of desperation like oily brass on my tongue, I stood, taut and trembling, waiting for Niamh to finish saddling the *zaiph*.

Chapter 20

BEYOND THE BLACK GATE

Suddenly, Siona spoke. Her words were said in a low, level voice, breathless and panting, but curiously flat and emotionless.

"You can never escape," she said.

I shrugged. "A man can but try."

"No, never. For my men will follow you to the world's end! To bring you back to me."

It was an odd choice of words.

"For your vengeance, I suppose. Or so you can sell us to the envoys of Ardha, our enemies."

She said nothing, but stood breathing quickly in the darkness.

Suddenly I staggered, as if a sudden fit of dizziness had come upon me. That feeling of weakness had grown steadily, until by now my head was whirling and my knees felt like rubber. I could not understand what was happening to me. The numbness which had so swiftly spread over my body, replacing the sting of Sligon's knife blow, made me feel cold and curiously feeble.

Siona stared at me through the gloom.

"You are hurt!" she breathed.

I shook my head, trying to clear it.

"It is nothing," I said sluggishly.

"No—you are wounded; Sligon got you!"

"A scratch—nothing more," I mumbled. Then, and louder, "Niamh. Hurry with the *zaiph*."

"Almost ready—another moment," the princess murmured from beyond us.

And then they were upon us, striking like silent wolves

130

out of the darkness. I whirled, sword ready, catching one blade in mid-air and wrenching it from the hand of the forester who wielded it. Another blade flickered—and another—and another. For one long moment I held three swordsmen at bay; but it was for a moment only.

Behind me, I heard Niamh cry out, and the sound of a blow being struck, and a man's hoarse bellow of pain. Then one of the foresters staggered out of the *zaiph* pens and fell sprawling with the mark of Niamh's blade across his face.

"Chong!" she cried. "Ready—come swiftly! They are all around us!"

But men encircled me and many swords flashed for my breast. With a terrific effort I beat them back, but the effort used much of the small store of strength that was left to me.

"Niamh! Mount and fly! I will follow."

"But—"

"*Fly*, my beloved!"

There came to my ears the drumming of great wings. A dark shape rose above us, blacker than the blackness. A heart-shaped face peered down at me through the murk, a girl's face white against the darkness. She was aloft! Thanks to whatever gods hold watch and ward over the World of the Green Star, she was aloft! And they could never catch her in this black gloom!

Or so, at least, I hoped. But I could do no more than I had done. A haze thickened before my eyes; my heart labored in my breast as if it would burst free of the cage of my ribs and fly to join her. Then I looked down and saw the spreading wetness across my chest, the red blood leaking from my severed arteries, pumping from the terrible wound just below my heart.

He had struck well, the hunched and sidling little traitor. Well, at least he had gone slinking before me down the road that led beyond the black gates of death. But I would follow soon after, that I knew.

The wound was mortal. No power in this world or another could save me now.

There was the sound of a woman weeping.

Siona bent over me, cradling me in her arms, her face distorted, twisted, wet with tears. I knew now why she had seemed so strange toward me, and why she had humiliated

Niamh in my presence. God help me, I never suspected it before, but the Amazon girl—*loved* me.

A momentary pang of despair went through me. Surely it could not end like this, surely the gods could not be so cruel, to take my life now when Niamh needed me most, when the armies of her enemies were already moving to march against defenseless Phaolon. I could not die here, leaving Niamh alone and lost and helpless in the great forest of world-tall trees. . . .

Again I glimpsed her white face through the gloom as she circled the branch. Her dark eyes were enormous against the pallor of her face. She could see the horrible stain of blood that drenched me from breast to mid-thigh; she knew that the chance blow struck by a cowardly traitor had laid low the hero of a thousand legends in the very moment when he was needed most. Oh, the irony of it! How the gods of this world must have laughed at the irony of my ending!

With my last strength I lifted my voice and called to her to be gone, to fly off into the night, to hide that her enemies might not find her. And a sort of madness came over me at the end; I wildly promised that she and I would meet again—that somewhere, somehow, I would come to her.

Through the darkness and the haze that thickened before my eyes I drank in my last look of her. But then she was gone, a dark figure fading into the darkness, gone from my fading vision all too soon, vanished into the trackless night.

Niamh, Niamh! Somehow, somewhere, we shall meet again. . . .

And then, as it comes to all men, however urgent their need for life, death came to me, and I began my long journey down that dark road to the gates from which there is no returning.

And so it is that the stories of most men reach their appointed ending.

But for me, the capricious Fates had reserved another, and a far more curious, ending.

In a way, I suppose it was a respite: but, in truth, this respite was far more cruel an ending to my story than the simple dignity of death could ever be.

I have said it already, that my tale is the strangest any

man has ever told, and that the adventures through which I have passed are like those no other man has ever experienced in all the labyrinth of the ages. This may sound like wild and outrageous boasting, but it is nothing else but honest truth.

I do not know why God or Fate or Chance, or whatever nameless and unknown Power rules over the fortunes of men, reserved for me the strange, unearthly miracle. I wish I did know, for without understanding the thing, I can learn nothing from it—nothing but sorrow, nothing but a pain that will not leave my heart—nothing but a question that haunts me night and day and will not let me rest.

A question to which I have no answer.

A question that may never be answered. . . .

But let me tell the thing exactly as it happened.

There was a darkness that was absolute, and a sleep that lasted forever.

And then, after an immeasurable lapse of time I was roused from that slumber which I had thought to be eternal. There was a hand that held a vial to my nostrils, a broken vial that lay in the wet folds of a handkerchief. I inhaled a pungent vapor that stung my nostrils and made me gag and cough.

And blurrily, through dim eyes, I could make out more.

There was a tall man in a long white coat who was bending over me. I could dimly make out his face—serious, thoughtful, a clean-shaven face with keen eyes and dark hair that grew white at the temples.

The shadows were clearing now. I could see beyond the tall man in the white coat who held the crushed vial of pungent chemical to my nostrils. Beyond him there was the plump, motherly figure of a woman who stood with a handkerchief to her face, wiping her eyes.

I seemed to recognize that woman. And beyond her were daylit windows through which I could just make out green, rolling, wooded hills that also had a haunting familiarity to them.

"He is coming out of it now, I think."

It was the tall man in the white coat who spoke. The language in which he spoke sounded curious to my ears, but oddly familiar at the same time. My brain was numb and sluggish, my mind dull and clogged as with the dregs

of some long nightmare. I struggled to understand what
was happening to me.

"Oh, thank God, doctor!"

It was the plump, middle-aged woman who spoke. Her
words, too, were at once strange and at the same time
familiar, as were her features. It seemed to me that I had
known that face and that voice somewhere, sometime, as
in another life. . . .

As in another life.

And just like that, it came to me.

I recognized the anxious voice of my housekeeper, and
her worried features.

And behind her, beyond the windows, I recognized that
landscape of rolling hills. Those were the familiar green
hills of Connecticut, and this was my house, and I—I yet
lived.

Or lived again!

The doctor turned away, depositing the wet handkerchief and the crushed vial on the night table. Then his
strong fingers fumbled at my wrist, seeking a feeble,
erratic pulse.

"Will he—live, doctor?" my housekeeper asked anx-
iously.

He frowned, counting the beats of my heart.

"He lives, but just barely. A good thing you called when
you did, ma'am. He would not have lasted very much
longer, without medical aid. We must get him into an
oxygen tent, and swiftly."

"But whatever happened! Whatever *is* it!"

He frowned thoughtfully, pursing his lips.

"I wish I could say! Something quite beyond my experience, I'm afraid. Some sort of trance and coma, but not
one induced by drugs or disease or injury, as far as I can
tell. But there's no time to waste in talk. You have a
telephone here, of course?"

"In the hall."

"Good. Let me call the hospital, have them get the
intensive care unit ready to receive a patient . . . I assume
there is somebody here—a gardener, a chauffeur—who
can help me get him downstairs?"

"Of course. I'll call Wagner. . . ."

They left me then. There were footsteps in the hall, the
sounds of a telephone being dialed. I lay, not moving a

muscle, pervaded by a weakness that went beyond the flesh to include the spirit as well. An ironic smile twisted my lips. I would have laughed, had I been able. For I understood in full at last the bitter jest the Gods or the Fates had arranged for me. Yes, it was clear now, all too terribly clear. The death of the *body* of the Lord Chong had not meant the death of my spirit but merely the extinguishing of my consciousness for a time, during which my far-wandering spirit-self escaped from its borrowed mansion of clay and fled back across the cold, dark gulfs between the stars to the world where my own true body lay empty and waiting to receive it.

In time I recovered my strength again, but there were many days when my spirit clung tenuously to my wasted flesh and only the iron strength of a trained and disciplined will helped me to keep my hold on life.

I had been absent from my body for far too long, you see ... far longer than I had expected to be, caught as I was in the swirl of events on a wonderful and alien world far distant from my own, a world that seems to me now but a peculiarly vivid and intensely realistic dream.

During the enforced leisure of my convalescence I have written down this record of my experiences on the World of the Green Star, impelled by an urgency I cannot quite name. Perhaps it is that I wish to remember everything as it was then, lest I forget the awe and beauty, the strangeness and terror, of that experience that must surely be the most weird and marvelous adventure ever lived by a denizen of this planet. This document shall be placed in a sealed vault, to be opened only in the event of my death; if ever curious eyes peruse these pages, I feel certain that this record will be termed nothing more than a work of extravagant fiction.

And now that I have reached the final ending of my story, I am aware of an odd reluctance to terminate it, as if by setting down those fatal words—*The End*—I am letting go of my adventure, thus permitting it to recede from me into the dim vistas of the past ... while I am doomed to live on into the future. While I yet toil on, page after page, my strange adventures and my distant friends are real and very near; but once the manuscript has been finished and set aside, the thing is over and done and ended.

Ere long, they tell me, my strength will have been fully

regained. I have dreamed many times of voyaging in spirit-form yet a second time across the dark cosmos to that strange world of eternal mists and towering trees and jewel-box cities. But what is there left for me to return to? I failed to save from the clutches of her mortal enemies the woman I love, who by now has surely suffered death at the hands of her enemies, whether at the hands of the tyrant Akhmim or of the vengeful Siona I cannot know.

Could I endure it, to go back to view the tomb of that dead loveliness? I do not need to venture there, for part of me lies therein as well. My heart is buried in the sepulcher of Niamh the Fair. . . .

Only the other day, browsing through an old, well-loved book, I found a set of verses that might have been set down for my eye alone, so intimately did they speak to my sorrow:

> *Up from Earth's Centre through the Seventh Gate*
> *I rose, and on the Throne of Saturn sate,*
>   *And many a Knot unravel'd by the Road;*
> *But not the Master-knot of Human Fate.*

Wise old Omar the Tent-maker! Did he guess somewhat of these matters, dreaming there by moonlight in the rose gardens of his native Persia? Who can say—who can know? For, whether it be by chance or accident or design, that verse plays upon a most peculiar coincidence.

"Up from Earth's Centre through the Seventh Gate . . ."

The old Tibetan mystics whose soul-science I employed to unlock the portals of the spirit, to loosen the bonds, to set my astral body free that it might flee this clay and soar aloft to strange and marvelous worlds that lay beyond the moon itself—those sages call by that very name the orifice through which my spirit fled—"the Seventh Gate"!

Through which my spirit fled to a fate stranger and more wonderful than I could ever have dreamed. To a life of glory and heroism and adventure beyond the wildest imaginings of the romancers. And to a love so precious that I feel it yet, in another body, on another world. A love that death cannot sever. . . .

Or *is* she dead? Lives she yet on that dim world of miracles that lies under the Green Star? Did Niamh make good her escape from the clutches of Siona's foresters, who would sell her to the envoys of her hated enemy,

Akhmim of Ardha? Is she lost and alone, wandering among the sky-tall trees, going every moment in peril, lacking my strong arm? Does she lie at this moment in chains in the dungeons of Akhmim, while her city and her kingdom lay down their swords and open the gates to the cruel hordes of the invader? Or did Siona save her for vengeance alone, to sit smiling while her fair flesh was torn beneath the knives of the torturers? Or did Niamh elude her pursuers, escape the savage predators of the giant trees, and find her way to the safety of her city of Phaolon? Perhaps at this very moment, the hordes of Ardha are locked in battle with the chivalry of Phaolon before the glittering gates of the Jewel City, while Niamh the Fair, armed like a warrior princess, leads her gallant soldiery against the foe . . . and I am here, *here,* unable to stand beside her in that last battle, and lend my strength and my sword to the defense of the woman I love and the kingdom that hailed me as its hero and savior!

It could be; it could well be. The last sight I had of her was as she flew off into the night, mounted upon the back of a fresh *zaiph.* Far could she have flown before the foresters of the Secret City could have mounted up and flown off in her pursuit. And in the ink-black night, in the moonless dark of the world of the giant trees, it would have been a mighty task to have found her, once she was flown.

Yes! she *could* have escaped! She could have lived to find her way to freedom! *She might be living at this hour. . . .*

Will I ever know?

Will we live and die worlds apart, never knowing the ending of the story?

Will *anyone* ever know?

It will be a time yet before my flesh and my spirit are strong enough to make their weird voyage of the soul across space between the stars a second time. *Will I voyage forth again to the World of the Green Star?*

I do not think so.

For how could I return to take my place beside the woman I love? The Lord Chong is dead. His body was cut down by the knife of a traitor. And from that second death his body will not rise, as from the first. And how could I return to claim the love of Niamh as—another man?

It is that which restrains me.

It would be torment unendurable to return to the World of the Green Star a bodiless spirit—to look upon events in which I could not partake—to gaze upon the unattainable loveliness of the Goddess-Queen whose lips I could never kiss, whose slim, vibrant body my arms could not hold.

And yet ... would that torture be any worse than the torment I suffer now, the torment of *not knowing?*

In truth, the Gods have played an ironic jest upon me. I died; I live again; and I must live on, and never know the ending of my own story!

The old Persian poet must have dreamed of my strange and terrible predicament, as he strolled there in the moon-lit gardens of his beloved Naishápúr so many centuries ago.

For as, musing, I read on in that old book of verses, I came at length to yet another quatrain he set down in golden Persia long ago: another verse that weirdly echoes the irony of my peculiar doom: another verse strangely meaningful to me alone of all men who have ever trod the dust of this Earth or read the pages of this book of song.

> I sent my Soul through the Invisible,
> Some Letter of that After-life to spell:
>   And by and by my Soul return'd to me,
>   And answer'd "I Myself am Heav'n and Hell."

And with those words I close this narrative.

AUTHOR'S NOTE

ON THE "BURROUGHS TRADITION"

On August 14, 1911, the opening portion of an unfinished novel by an otherwise unknown writer living in Chicago was mailed to the offices of *All-Story Magazine* at 175 Fifth Avenue in New York. Tom Metcalf, the managing editor, liked it, and wrote back ten days later suggesting it be lengthened. The author of the story, a thirty-six-year-old Chicagoan, quickly complied. He had failed at several business ventures, having tried his hand at running a stationery store, a mail-order business selling pots and pans, and working as an accountant for Sears, Roebuck; at the moment, he was eking out a meager income selling patent medicine through ads in pulp magazines. A month later he returned the manuscript to Metcalf, now 63,000 words long, and collected his check for $400.

In time the story appeared in print. It was serialized in six installments, and the first of these was published in the February, 1912, issue of *All-Story*. The world has never quite been the same since.

The author had called it *Dejah Thoris, Martian Princess*, but Metcalf changed the title to the more romantic and exciting *Under the Moons of Mars*. Through a slight mixup, the serial version appeared under a pen name, Norman Bean. When A. C. McClurg & Co. published the story as a hardcover book in October, 1917, the title reached its final form as *A Princess of Mars*, and the author's real name appeared in the by-line. His name, of course, was Edgar Rice Burroughs.

That $400 check launched one of the most phenomenal

careers in the history of the novel. From the obscurity of an absolutely unknown business failure who turned to writing adventure stories for the pulp magazines, Edgar Rice Burroughs became almost overnight an astonishing success. His magazine serials were turned into books which sold millions of copies all over the world and are still in print and selling today. Movies were made from them as early as 1917: today, at least forty-two feature films and serials have been adapted from his literary creations, and there has also been a radio program or two and a television series. Burroughs' characters very quickly began appearing in the Sunday comic sections of the nation's leading newspapers. The original "Tarzan" page, drawn by Hal Foster, who was later to create "Prince Valiant" and to become one of the two or three greatest artists in the history of the comics, launched a series that became an historic milestone in comic art and continues today, under another hand, in the Sunday pages and in monthly comic books.

Before long, Burroughs became the most popular science fiction writer in the world, outselling Sir Arthur Conan Doyle and even nudging the immortal H. G. Wells to a secondary place in the esteem and affection of the reading public. He founded his own publishing company to print his own books, and when he died at the age of seventy-four he had written some sixty-five books or so and was a millionaire many times over. Almost any way you want to look at it—from the standard of his earnings, his immense and worldwide popularity, or the permanence of his work, which has thus far enchanted and charmed four generations of readers and movie audiences— Burroughs was one of the most successful writers who ever lived: quite possibly *the* most successful writer.

He is, of course, snubbed by all the college literary professors, the librarians, the schoolteachers, the critics and historians of literature, who put him down as a "mere entertainer" and a lowly pulp hack, unworthy of their consideration. (These people never change: their grandfathers were saying exactly the same thing about Robert Louis Stevenson, Alexander Dumas, Sir Walter Scott and Rudyard Kipling; the academic mind is always uneasy when dealing with an artist who makes money.) But such "official" neglect makes no difference. Millions of readers have succumbed to the magic of Edgar Rice Burroughs, and that magic is still alive and just as powerful as ever. I cannot conceive of an era in which his superb adventure stories could fail to enchant and delight new generations.

I was a twelve-tear-old boy, living in St. Petersburg, Florida, when I first discovered him. I had read my way shelf by shelf around the walls of the children's room, devouring the Oz books, Doctor Dolittle, Mary Poppins, and Andrew Lang's "color fairy books." I was in the mood for more solid and satisfying fare—if possible!—so I ventured into the alcove set aside for teen-agers. It was generally a dismal corner, given over to extinct writers and dead books, like *Silas Marner* and *The House of The Seven Gables,* but some kindly benefactor, or some wise librarian who really understood boys, had installed a long shelf full of rather fat books in durable, worn library bindings. This shelf came just about to my twelve-year-old eye level, and, glancing along the row, my eye fastened on one title in particular: *The Master Mind of Mars.*

I checked it out—I took it home—and all the long trolley car ride home I read it—and all that long, lazy, unforgettable summer afternoon I was deep in its pages. All that warm summer day I galloped across the dead sea bottoms of Barsoom, under the glory of the hurtling moons, my longsword slapping against my bare thigh, battling a horde of foes for the love of the most beautiful princess of two worlds.

I was a goner from that first moment, a helpless captive from the first page on. And today I bless the memory of the unknown person who set that book within my reach. . . .

The book you hold in your hands is really a sort of love letter. A love letter written to a man dead now for twenty-three years, a man I never knew and never even met, but who changed my life and the lives of millions like me. For there have been millions, like that little boy I once was, on that lazy summer afternoon thirty years ago, who have ridden their trusty *thoat* over the dead sea bottoms, under the hurtling moons, battling through the marble cities of ancient Mars, with Kantos Kan and Tars Tarkas and faithful Woola at their side.

Some of them became writers themselves when they grew up. The "Burroughs tradition" had its followers even in Burroughs' own time, like Roy Rockwood and Otis

Adelbert Kline, the Rex Beach who wrote *Jaragu of the Jungle*, and the Ray Cummings who wrote *Tama of the Light Country*. But the deepest, most sincere contributions to the genre Burroughs founded are those that have been written by those of us who encountered his work as youngsters and grew up to follow in his footsteps.

For example, without *Tarzan of the Apes* I do not think James Blish would ever have written *The Night Shapes*, nor would it have been possible for Philip José Farmer to have written *Lord of the Trees* or *Time's Last Gift* or *Lord Tyger*. Certainly, it would have been impossible for Fritz Leiber to ever write his *Tarzan and the Valley of Gold*.

And without John Carter of Mars and Carson of Venus, Andre Norton would probably have written books of a very different sort, perhaps Civil War romances for teen-agers; and surely Leigh Brackett would never have written her own splendidly entertaining Martian and Venusian fantasies. Nor would Michael Resnick have written *Goddess of Ganymede*, nor John Norman his *Tarnsman of Gor* and its sequels, nor Michael Moorcock his Martian trilogy. Nor would I have written *Under the Green Star* or my new Jandar of Callisto trilogy, which should be coming into print from another publisher shortly after you read these words.

There are those who like Tarzan best, or Pellucidar, or Carson of Venus. For me, however, the Mars books won my heart when I was a boy, and I have never cared to ask for it back. But even as a youngster there were some things Burroughs did in his stories that bothered and annoyed me. He was really an admirable writer in many ways, and he possessed an amazing gift for the fantastic adventure story and a truly first-rate imaginative genius, but even Homer has been known to nod and Shakespeare himself had his off-days.

It always flummoxed me, for instance, that when John Carter flew to Mars in astral form he left his physical body behind in that Arizona cave—but by the time he got to Mars, he had his body again, steely thews and cool gray eyes and everything. Even as a kid, this annoyed me! Since then, I have come to understand and forgive: *A Princess of Mars* was, after all, his first novel, and he was still technically an amateur when he wrote it.

Well, I am no longer an amateur and this is not my first

novel—*Under the Green Star* is, in fact, my thirtieth novel—so, in taking my hero to the World of the Green Star in his spirit-form, I took considerable pains to explain how he acquired a body once he got there.

Those readers who are familiar with the flavor of Burroughs' prose will, I think, notice that *Under the Green Star* is written in quite a different style. While my Jandar of Callisto books are written in a close approximation of Burroughs' own prose style, that just sort of happened. I have learned by now that each book has a style all its own and that the wisest thing the writer can do is to give his book free rein and let it find the style in which it feels most comfortable. *Under the Green Star* seemed to want a crisp, vivid style *à la* A. Merritt's prose, and who was I to say "no" to it?

Readers in the know will also realize that the World of the Green Star is nothing at all like Barsoom. Burroughs' Mars is a dying world of ocher deserts: the World of the Green Star is a lush forest world teeming with fantastic life, covered with towering, mighty trees. This, too, sort of just happened, but I was not so much trying to imitate the Mars books as I was trying to pay tribute to the immense imaginative talent which created them: I was trying to write a Burroughs *kind* of story, rather than just a Burroughs story.

The difference, I think, is that which lies between *imitation* and *influence*. Some writers have tried to *imitate* Burroughs and they have usually fallen flat on their faces, or on another portion of the anatomy. Other writers have more wisely permitted themselves to be *influenced* by Burroughs, and such experiments have often paid off by producing remarkably good books, as I think John Norman's "Gor" books are remarkably good books, and Philip José Farmer's *The Wind Whales of Ishmael*. When he turned the screenplay of *Tarzan and the Valley of Gold* into a novel, Fritz Leiber did not in the least try to imitate Burroughs, especially not in the matter of prose style; and, again, the result was a remarkably good book that can stand on its own feet. I would like to think that *Under the Green Star* belongs in this same category; I hope so, anyway.

Such books as *Under the Green Star* are best written during a period of serenity and freedom from worries, out of love and nostalgia. I'm afraid *Under the Green Star* was written under considerable stress and strain, during a period that was not the happiest time of my life. I hope this does not show, and I hope the book does not suffer from the troubled times during which it was written. Because I enjoyed the writing of it very much, and I would like to do another book of this kind again, sometime soon.

But whether or not that happens is really up to you, who have read it, and, of course, to Donald A. Wollheim, who has published it, and who permitted me to go three weeks beyond my deadline in order to write it the way it should be written.

—LIN CARTER

Hollis, Long Island, New York